Roots X Roots

Bloodthirsty

Angelique Inostine

Contents

1

BASE

May 6, 2011

The first time I tasted blood was the day I fell in love. The deliciousness of privilege was finger-licking good. I wouldn't say I'm a fiend, but I have an insatiable sour tooth. The more I resist it, the more I want it. I wasn't looking for love, it splattered on me. I'll never forget the day. Brynn was twelve, and it was the last class of the day in sixth-grade science. The teacher wrote the homework on the whiteboard. There weren't any assigned seats, but David and Ian usually sat together. Those two always got in trouble for laughing and playing. Our teacher, Mrs. Cinderella Kruger, was pretty patient with them. They were the only two that acted out in class. Everyone else was too scared that her name had a double meaning, and she might kill them in their dreams for misbehaving on some revenge shit. That day, David wasn't in class, so Ian sat behind Brynn. For the life of me, I couldn't figure out how one of the only five white kids in our school *happened* to be in that class and *happened* to sit behind us. Ian hadn't paid attention all class, but suddenly he tapped on Brynn's shoulder, "Can you move to the back of the classroom?"

Brynn turned around with the sole intention of him seeing her eyes roll. He tapped her again, "Your hair is in my way. I can't see the board."

Brynn had a high donut bun with laid baby hair, and she hated being tapped. She turned around again.

"You don't even take notes. You can pretend to write the homework for your friend when you leave." Ian huffed and mumbled something under his breath.

Mrs. Kruger gave him a look and he got quiet. After class was over and all of the students left, Mrs. Kruger asked Brynn to stay behind. She knew that even though Brynn acted like she was okay, she was hurt. The embarrassment sat on her face like a black eye. Mrs. Kruger walked over to Brynn's desk, and rubbed her back,

"You okay, sweetie?"

Brynn looked up into her teacher's honey-brown eyes. "Yeah, I'm fine."

"What he said was offensive, and you have the right to be upset."

The loudspeaker came on, calling Mrs. Kruger to the front office. She wasn't gone more than thirty seconds before Ian returned to the classroom, acting as if he'd left something. We had open front desks back then, so he stuck his hand in it and reached around, grabbing air, then hitting the sides. Of course, it was empty. He was still behind Brynn when he leaned toward her and said,

"Tomorrow, I'm bringing my scissors." I took that as a threat.

You have to understand I was young, like Brynn. Even younger because I don't remember the years before. You could say I had been born yesterday, so that's how I responded. I lashed out. I overreacted. I didn't think twice. I had the unmitigated gall like that of a newborn vampire from Twilight and the propensity of a Symbiote. I was uncontrollable. I didn't evaluate the risk. I needed him to feel physical pain equal to the mental pain he'd caused me with that threat. I was hurt, scared, angry. That's when I struck him. As I said, the day I fell in love, it wasn't on purpose. I intended the payback, it was the blood I didn't expect. But he was all up in my space, making threats that I couldn't ignore. I smacked him across the mouth for uttering such disrespectful words. His chunky pale cheeks jiggled with vindication. But that wasn't enough. I didn't feel satisfied. Right before his very gaze, I became a beast, a creature of revenge. Things were about to get hairy.

With the brute force of a nine-tailed fox and resemblance of such, I struck him. Jab after jab, back-to-back. Appendages flew every which way, simultaneously hitting him. I punched him in the head. It bobbled back and forth. I hit him with a hook. His body jerked right. Another hook. His body jerked left. He didn't have time to think, no less respond. His arms dangled. His legs buckled. His body curved inward in retreat. It was the last hit that did it—the uppercut. He immediately lost consciousness. Blood shot from his nose and landed on me as he flew across the room like a limp noodle. That's when the *flavor* hit. When his lanky body smashed into the wall, I watched the posters fall. I took that as a white flag. Of course, I was taken aback, but as his life force gushed out, it entered me. I took it upon myself, I reveled in it, and I could breathe. Something about it felt right even though I knew it was wrong. I had to protect Brynn because when it comes to protecting herself, she's a little passive. She was speechless. She stood there for a while. Eyes wide. She stared at his neck for a heartbeat but didn't bother to actually check. She grabbed her book bag and hurried out of the classroom before Mrs. Kruger returned. We were in a trailer on the side of the school. It was one of those long and narrow kinds. The school refers to them as mobile classrooms. The only thing mobile about them is how easy it is to get in and out.

Usually, Brynn would take the bus home but that day she couldn't. Not with all the blood in her hair and all over her bubblegum pink shirt. She snuck out of the trailer, avoiding the school buses and people out front. Home was within walking distance. She took the beaten path through some trees that sat between the school and our neighborhood. The wind whistled into Brynn's ear. It was hard to hear, no less think, so, she turned her head slightly to quiet the sound. She exhaled, the noise of bus engines and screaming children was mostly silenced on the other side of the trees. It was calm and quiet. The neighbors were still at work. And thank goodness for that, because most of them recognized us. She could focus on the birds singing. She could hear herself think but only long enough to realize what had just happened. She burst into tears, upset about what Ian had said. Upset that her hair got in the way.

Brynn speed walked down the street not just to get home quickly, but to avoid the smell of that Bradford Pear tree up ahead. They're often mistaken for cherry blossoms because of their white flowers, but the difference is the smell. You know, those ones that smell like a perm. She wiped the blood from her chubby cheeks. Her mom used to say she looked like she was storing food for the winter. Brynn hated it, but those cheeks added character to her big smile. We made it home. She stood in front of the two-story house and stared at the bluish-grey front door, knowing her mother was inside. She wanted to gather the courage for what she was about to do.

But that was then. This is now. It's been nine years since the day I fell in love. I never forgot the flavor or the taste of revenge. I did forget the details though, until August 16, 2020, when a shock of hair brought the memory back to life for me. That same day, in August, I slaughtered a man. I know you're wondering who I am. What's going on? I'm getting there, but let me be straight up. You know that person inside of you that must be kept on lock because if they get out of control, you will lose your job, your family, your life, and your friends. At any moment, I could flip. That's who I am. I'm just keeping it real. I'm the shield for her mind, the protector for her body, and the crown of her soul. I'm her confidence, her identity, and her strength. I'm her hair.

The privileged were unaware of my crimps. Every time they judged me, every time they touched me, every time I had to pretend to be more like them, my heart shrank. That's why I needed *it*. The way I saw it is this: if they're going to take my heart, then the least they can do is pay in blood. That's how I thrived. I was already dead on the outside. That was an everyday thing. That was the norm, the shaft I was given. If I died on the inside, too, I'd be like them, empty and love-lacked. That went against everything I was, every reason I existed. What purpose would I have served? I will say this, though, even in death, I looked damn good. Once, I was fine, but we won't go there.

I considered myself pretty and relaxed, but a bit sensitive, too. I'll admit that. I wore my emotions on my sleeve—no secrets to hide. Hell, I couldn't have hidden anything if I tried. That wasn't me. When we were out, people always stared. I know what they were probably thinking. How does she do it? They wanted to be me. They wanted to feel me. They said I look exotic. Honey, please, I looked just like everybody else. Well, I tried to, anyway. It was a constant battle, but I worked with what I had. I wanted to fit in, look good, and be liked, like everybody else... But not anymore. Anyway, I could talk about myself all day, but this story isn't about me. I was just a means to an end. I sit upon the throne of Brynn Reaux Brown. People always mispronounced her middle name. She liked to joke and say, "I may be brown and thick like gravy, but it's pronounced row, not roo." The girl had spunk. She had a heart of rose gold. Her purpose in life was to help people. She couldn't help herself. On the other hand, I would've done anything to safeguard her. I sound like I'm in control but that's not the whole truth. Our struggles look different, but our duties are aligned. We go about it differently, but we want the same thing. She was all rainbows, glitter, and pink shit. She smiled, kept her emotions in check, and followed the rule: if you don't have anything nice to say then don't.... yadda, yadda, blah, blah bullshit. Not me. You can miss me with the bullshit. I wouldn't have considered her to be submissive or timid, but you didn't have to tell her to mind her manners or watch her tone. Those were the rules, and she was already following them.

I have an invested interest in Brynn. For the most part, she took care of me, and I did my best to take care of her, too, even if she didn't always know it. Or agree. At times, she pulled me in tight but occasionally, she let me down. I know she loved me, but sometimes she neglected me. When I spoke, she didn't hear me. Literally, she couldn't hear me. Nonetheless, I played my part. Try not to be alarmed by the things I'm saying. The point is, you never know what you're going to get. Today I'm blunt, and tomorrow? It's my tone. Next, I'd be dry. You may not like me, but you can't miss me. I'm the bold one. Call me Brair, short for Brynn's hair. But wait, how could hair be talking? Well, the question isn't how, but why? The answer is that I have something to say. I'm tired of laying down. I'm tired of being complicit. I want to stand up. I want to be wild and free, loose and crinkly. I want to breathe.

April 24, 2020

Doctor appointments suck. Hell, dentist appointments do too. Everything you've been neglecting on your body is brought to the light, literally. It's either a light in your mouth or a light in your cooch. They'll tell you that you need to floss and how dropping a few pounds would do you some good. There are no hiding secrets from the doctor. The truth is in the pudding. Brynn had been avoiding this appointment like the plague because the doctor always wanted to stick fingers in places unmentioned. She was only twenty-one, and I thought they didn't check that stuff until you were fifty, at least. It felt like we were waiting forever. As much as she hated hearing about how she should exercise more, she hated waiting even more. Time is a commodity, and thinking back, I wasn't sure how much we had. Brynn was nervous. There was a shelf of brochures staring her in the face. Mental health treatments, STD, blood pressure, you name it. She couldn't help but read the front of them all. It was a compulsion that served the purpose of keeping her mind occupied. A boring compulsion, I might add. I would have preferred we scroll Facebook. So, I couldn't help but get excited when the nurse called her name, "Brynn Brown... Can you leave a sample?" With a clipboard in one hand, the nurse opened the door to the bathroom with her other, "Write your name on the cup first, then come to room number three when you're done."

Brynn mumbled, "Uhh, thanks." The door slammed behind her.

When we got to the room, a disposable gown was already waiting. She removed her violet skinny jeans and hot pink racerback shirt to put on the gown. Brynn started to complain. *What are these things called anyway? They're so big and useless. My titties be on the loose, flopping around. I feel so naked and vulnerable.* I could hear her thoughts. More waiting. More staring at dull, lifeless paintings. What was wrong with being colorful anyway? A bit of color never hurt anybody. These walls needed character. It could've livened the place up a bit. Brynn could hear Dr. McIntosh rustling on the other side of the door. Brynn sat straight and uncrossed her legs. She didn't want the doctor to think she was a slouch. The doctor knocked once and floated in, rushing but somehow angelic.

"Hi, Brynn. How are you?"

"Hello. I'm fine," Brynn didn't bother reciprocating the concern. She wanted to get straight to the point.

The doctor clickity-clacked on the keyboard. "I had them put you in a gown because I want to redo your pap smear and possibly an ultrasound. Your results from the last pap came back abnormal."

"Okay. Well, I've had some spotting and heavy periods."

Not responding immediately, the doctor rolled on her stool to a drawer for gloves. She then pulled out the stirrups, guiding Brynn's feet into them. Finally, she spoke. "Understood. Due diligence."

The initial pause had Brynn worried. "What could be wrong?"

"It could be nothing, or it could be a benign growth. Lay back. Let's take a look." She slid the light closer to see better. The heat radiated. Brynn thought *too much lube—such an awkward experience.*

Brynn broke the awkward silence. "Could it be cancer?"

"Everything could be anything. Let's not jump to conclusions. Take a deep breath for me, please."

There she went again, down the hollow rabbit hole of Brynn's head. *What does she mean everything could be anything? I know she has an idea. They always do. What if it's cancer? Omigod, I'm too young to die. I don't even have kids yet. I want one, at least. I need to experience that unconditional love. Maybe it's something simple, like a yeast infection.*

"You can sit up now. We'll have to send your pap swab out for testing, but I'd like to get you set up for an ultrasound."

"Another appointment?" She didn't take kindly to the idea of more waiting. Neither did I.

"We have an ultrasound tech in-house. We can do it today."

"Oh, ok." Now, she sounded disappointed. She would have preferred not knowing for just a bit longer. Pretending things were perfect for another week or two wouldn't have killed her. Or maybe it would have. What felt like an eternity later, the ultrasound was completed, and the doctor returned. She didn't sit this time. "Do you know your family's medical history? Specifically, your mother or sisters, if you have siblings?"

"Don't have a sister and my mom... Well, no. Not really. Why?"

"It looks like uterine fibroids, but as I said, we'll send the swab for extensive testing."

"Or it could be cancer?"

"Does cancer run in your family?"

"Yes. That's what most of them die from. Stomach cancer, pancreatic cancer, prostate cancer. I don't even know all the cancers."

"Noted." The doctor clicked her pen even though she wrote nothing.

"Okay, what can I do in the meantime?" Brynn asked.

"Well, I've been seeing you for years, so this is off the record when I say this..."

"Okaaaay." Brynn tilted her head to the side.

"Woman to woman, I was watching a documentary recently, and they believe relaxers are linked to reproductive conditions like infertility and fibroids. This is especially true for Black women since you all are at an increased risk of fibroids. Over time, relaxers may also contribute to alopecia, and only God knows what else."

I knew Becky and her good hair couldn't have been saying what I thought she was saying. If Brynn stopped perming, she wouldn't have her powers. Since I exist because of the perms, then I would've died without them. I'd be gone forever—hard pass.

The doctor continued, "I know I have no right to advise it, but…"

"Okay, then, don't," I said, as if she could hear me.

"Maybe you might consider going natural. Those products have nasty chemicals and toxins that enter your bloodstream through the follicle openings in your hair and skin, especially if you've experienced something like burning or scarring. These toxins show up in blood, breast milk, and urine. They starve your hair of oxygen and nutrients, which can also cause breathing issues. I bet your hair is craving nourishment. It's the first line of defense against relaxers."

Oh my! Could that be why I craved blood—the oxygenated and nutrient-rich blood of those with the privilege of never having had a relaxer? Brynn tussled with the idea in her mind. *My hair? It's the bane of my existence but also the beauty of my face. It's my womanhood. It never does what I want, but I don't think I could go natural. I'd be lost. We have a love-hate relationship. One I wouldn't trade to save the world.* That's what Brynn thought of me. What a backhanded compliment.

Brynn chuckled at the doctor, "Easier said than done."

"Don't get me wrong, I understand. If someone asked me to stop dying my hair, I would lose it, but if you want kids someday… a family, you might consider it. Do your research."

"You're saying I won't be able to have kids?"

"Studies haven't been done to prove anything. I'd never admit I said this, but we don't know everything there is to know about the human body. I will say this. The container suggests that pregnant women not use relaxers." Dr. McIntosh raised her eyebrows and tilted her head, looking at Brynn.

"Okay, I'll watch a documentary or something" Brynn agreed reluctantly.

"I also recommend clean eating and managing stress levels."

Brynn pressed her lips together. She thought, *if I don't have anything nice to say, then I won't say anything at all. That's the rule, right?*

"I know, I know. Easier said than done, but you must try for your own sake."

"I hear you, Dr. McIntosh."

"Stop at the front desk to make a follow-up appointment."

Brynn left without making that follow-up. Surprisingly though, she went home and watched three documentaries. The things we saw were wild. Tell me why this hair product caused a woman to have hearing problems? This is what happened. At first, she noticed her hair was brittle and thin. Then, she had allergic breakouts, her palms would turn red, and her periods only lasted a day. Eventually, her hair started falling out in clumps. We watched as she sifted through almost a dozen sandwich bags of her hair, each bag equated to a day of hair loss. It was so sad. Was that going to be me? Imagine, I'm stuffed into little sandwich bags, silenced. To make matters worse, the woman dealt with impaired speech, memory loss, and ringing ears. She couldn't sleep because the ringing was so bad. Sometimes, she said, it sounded like she was underwater. When a doctor finally prescribed her hearing aids, we witnessed her get choked up because, for the first time in a year, she could hear silence. You can't even hear silence. But seriously think about that for a second. That's maddening. I'd go crazy. Brynn hadn't experienced any of these things, so did we really need to worry? I guess if she might have fibroids, then technically, she is experiencing something. Anyway, back to this documentary. Another lady said she submitted an FDA report, describing convulsions, migraines, and skin ulcers but they told her that she was misusing the emergency line. If I had a face, it would've been cocked sideways. I couldn't believe it. I didn't want to believe it. And get this. A former chemist from a major hair company said instead of testing, they would wait for someone to be affected by these hair products. This man had the nerve to say that they waited for people to form a social media group saying their hair was falling out and their skin was on fire. That's how they found out about a problem. If they could be anything in this world, I need them to be fucking-for-real. But wait, there's more. There is no law requiring hair companies to test their products for safety. Umm, what?

There were many other stories and Brynn felt bad for each one. The scenes kept replaying in her mind. *How could these companies be allowing this?* She was disgusted. I was disgusted, but I couldn't have imagined losing myself, my consciousness. On the flip side, I couldn't have imagined Brynn going through what these women went through. I was starting to think that maybe she should go natural. Then I changed my mind just as quickly. I needed my creamy crack. I would've shriveled up and died without it. We'd been perming for years and we'd been good. Heck, I'd say we were better than good, since you know, we had powers and all. We were different. Those bad things wouldn't happen to us. Couldn't happen to us. Brynn thought: *I'm sure it's all good under the hood. I can't go natural. Then again, I'm hurting myself by keeping these powers. It would help me, but what about all of the people I help? Relaxers are my saving grace. Maybe God can fix me. Dear God, I know I don't go to church often, but can you please cure me? Well, being natural can't be that bad. Lots of Black women are doing it now.*

Brynn was back and forth with this. Heck, so was I. She was right. She wouldn't have me, Brair. I wouldn't be able to protect her. We wouldn't be able to help the world. Helping others was her obsession. Well, that and the color pink.

I want kids, and I don't want to ruin that for my future. Maybe I shouldn't. What if people call me ugly?

I agreed that she shouldn't. We were beautiful already and I wanted to keep it that way.

They'll whisper mean things when I walk by, like when I was a kid. I don't even remember my hair before perming. My mom used to keep it braided. She was so creative. I wish she were here. I wish I could remember her more. It's like I can see her, but she's blurry. Is that how all memories work? Ugh!

My memories were blurry too. Maybe it's because we share the same head.

I wonder if I'll have to wear an afro while it's growing out. My hair will definitely be in the way with an afro. Didn't men wear afros? How can something unisex be attractive? Men like long, straight hair, something that they can run their fingers through.

She was on her own with that one. I'm just saying. Don't touch me.

If I'm natural, wouldn't it defeat the purpose of going natural if I can't even find a man to have babies with? I'll look like a troll. "None shall pass," Brynn said in a deep mocking voice. *I'm already Black, and that comes with enough shit. Now, I would stand out even more. I'd be unsightly, grotesque to society.*

"You're right. We would be dick-repellent. Don't do it. Reconsider." She didn't hear me, of course. I'm always talking to myself.

3
MANE POWER

April 25, 2020

The hair salon sat in the midst of an old warehouse hub on Metropolitan Pkwy, renovated as a rental space for business owners. The rows of warehouses look like half a slave ship from an aerial view. I kid you not. Pulling up felt like driving yourself into a back alley robbery. From the outside, you wouldn't think the inside was so beautiful. Old roll-up garage doors were replaced with modern overhead glass garage doors. Others were replaced with simple double glass doors. Either way, it was a fancy upgrade that allowed for natural light. It had an avant-garde look that new-generation companies seem to cherish. Inside, the ceilings sat twenty feet high with white support beams peppered about, and the original brick, flaws and all, remained. The cracks were prevalent, but they gave the salon a homey feel. It was a hidden gem. On the walls hung monochrome portraits of Senator Kamala Harris, Frederick Douglass, Booker Taliaferro Washington, Bob Marley, Rosa Parks, and Reverend Dr. Martin Luther King, Jr. In the sitting area, above a black leather couch, a mural is painted on the wall of two hands touching to form the shape of a heart, the left purple, and the right green. The stylist's stations were minimalistic, with square mirrors and black leather chairs. It added to the contrast, the Feng shui. *By Your Side* was playing by Sade. She's a whole vibe.

As we sit, once again in Almara's chair, I'm greeted by a smell similar to that of burnt hair, lemongrass shampoo, and the unmistakable smell of ammonia. The relaxer. Almara walked toward her station dressed in all black. The sun slow-stroked her toffee skin. It shimmered from the sun –melanin poppin'. She sashayed with *swagger*. Every bit of fat jiggled in all the right places. She rocked a layered pixie cut, perfectly messy but always straight at the roots like she had a fresh perm. Consider her the younger auntie type that you can gossip with but she'll tell you like it is. Straight talk, tough love. She signaled for Brynn to come to the chair.

"Lean back for me," Almara pulled out a fairly used burgundy cape and draped it over Brynn, a little ripped on the collar but effective, nonetheless. Brynn watched as it dropped over her lap like a falling parachute. Almara lifted me in the back and fastened the cape to Brynn's neck. Brynn hated having to be there for hours at a time, but getting a perm every month was a must. Besides looking good, she needed the power. Who else was going to heal and protect our people? Her friends, family, and even the guys at the homeless shelter. They needed her help. She vowed to help them be better, to save their lives. That was her purpose. That's what she believed she was put on Earth to do. She must've gotten lost in her thoughts for too long because Almara asked,

"Who got you zoned out like that? Was it that snack that dropped you off?"

He is a snack, ain't he? I could eat him up. That man is the definition of handsome. That supple brown skin is like catnip, and he stays at the gym. Fine ass, looking like a football player. All I do is dream about him –waking up from the pulsations, sopping wet. I bet it's big too. Whew! Snap out of it. I'm taken. I have Marc.

Brynn chuckled so that Almara didn't know she was right. "Oh, Jacqori. It's nothing like that. We're just friends. I was thinking about some volunteer work I need to do in a few weeks."

"Where's Marc? Why didn't he drop you off?"

"He's been acting funny. He ain't never there when I need him. Like today, my car is in the shop, and my birthday is in three days. I texted him yesterday asking for a ride here. He said he got me but never showed up. I called and texted him multiple times. Still no answer, so I texted Cory. He responded immediately."

"Cory?"

"My bad. That's what I call Jacqori."

"You know how I feel about that. There's plenty of fish in the sea. Dump his ass." Almara parted Brynn's hair with a rat tooth comb. Brynn wriggled in the chair, trying to get more comfortable. The bell on the door dinged as a lady walked in with a shirt that read, "*This is my happy place.*" Almara smacked her teeth, "Another one bites the dust. Then they got the nerve to come up in her for help because they don't know what to do with their hair." Almara was always going in on someone's hair. I guess that came with the territory.

"Who are you talking about?" Brynn asked like she didn't just see the lady come in.

"Happy place over there. You didn't see that rag-doll come in? You can't miss her. Hair all matted up and dry. The lengths ain't even the same. It looks like she let a dog chew on the ends. This ain't her happy place, since it looks like she ain't been to a salon in years, no less even touched her hair in weeks."

Brynn laughed to mask her discomfort. "Maybe she's trying to go natural."

"Everybody's been jumping on that bandwagon." Almara intensely applied petroleum to Brynn's scalp. "If they keep that up, I'll be broke in no time."

"I mean, I heard it was better for your hair."

Almara grabbed three banana clips. "What's better for your hair is getting it done regularly by a professional. Going natural is just a journey to split ends and a nappy mess," she said sharply.

"Even if the doctor suggested it?"

Almara stopped what she was doing and spun Brynn toward the mirror. "I know you ain't thinking about going natural?"

Brynn looked away, hoping to be spun back around. "My doctor said perms could be causing me to get uterine fibroids."

Almara turned toward another stylist's station. She had wooden letters above the mirror that read, "Christine." They made eye contact with each other as if to say "*Can you believe this shit?*"

"Girl, your doctor is an idiot. What yo' hair got to do with yo' ovaries? You need to find a new doctor."

Almara thought she was so smart. "Uh, it's the uterus, smart girl." I tried to correct her. I don't know why I bothered because she didn't listen. Well, she couldn't. But if she could, she wouldn't have anyway.

"A thought is just a thought, right?" Brynn tried to convince Almara because she hated tension, but it wasn't just a thought. It was a treatment plan. It was something she needed to do for her health, yet here she was, getting another perm against the doctor's advice. She wasn't ready. Neither was I.

"If you say so, but you can't go natural." Almara grabbed the relaxer and made a snarky comment. Her tone went from condescending to vindictive. "It ain't like you can get your powers anywhere else."

Brynn had been getting her hair done by Almara since she was twelve. Almara said that her perm had magical effects and there was none like it anywhere else. I didn't know how the perm gave Brynn powers but what I know is that I was born around that same timeframe. Brynn knew that suddenly she could do things with her hair. Mostly stupid, simple things at first, like using me to get the remote or hold a cup to her mouth. Once, I helped her clean her room. It was a hot mess. Stuffed animals were strewn about, clothes were on the floor. Nothing was in its place. Because she would have rather played video games than clean, I split into elongated wisps of hair to hasten the process. There must've been fifty pieces of me moving things about the room. It was clean in mere minutes, but it took a toll. She wasn't just fatigued, her sight became blurry and she started to hallucinate. She had narcolepsy levels of tiredness. There was no fighting sleep. We woke up on the floor three hours later.

Instantly, Almara started talking normally again, like she didn't just have an attitude. "Anyway, what style did you want today?"

"I'm thinking something basic but cute, like a blunt cut bob, with a front middle part. I like the color. Keep it jet black."

"Going for the gusto?"

"I want that home-wrecker hair." Brynn asserted.

"Uh uh. Don't do that." Almara didn't like that connotation.

As she applied the perm to my roots, I felt euphoric. Things got blurry, and I would've sworn the room was spinning. Kamala's eyes moved in the picture on the wall, she smiled at me. The colors in the salon started to blend and swirl. Everything got dark and Almara's voice sounded distorted. It was trippy, always is, always has been. I can't say I hate it. Just call me a creamy crackhead.

"I ain't say I *was* wrecking homes. I want to look like I might."

"So, you want to look like a ho? I got you. Say less."

"I ain't say all that."

"Last I checked, ain't no homewrecker without a ho."

"You can't judge a book by its cover, Almara."

"I can, and I will. Hair is the best judge of character. Before our hair was shaved off as slaves, Black hair signified class and status. You can walk out of the house looking regular-degular, but if your hair ain't on point, everything else gets canceled out. Hair says everything I need to know about a person... You can tell how much money they make, what kind of car they drive, and if they're single or taken. You can tell if they got kids and if they've let go a bit. You can sense confidence. You can tell if they wrap their hair at night. Rough sex, maybe. Bedhead, maybe. Folks always think it's the shoes on their feet or the clothes on their back. Anybody can buy a pair of red bottoms, but everybody can't take the time to have good hair. So yeah, I can judge a book by its cover because your hair defines you."

Oh my! Is she still talking? When I came to, pieces of me were gone, and though I didn't look like it, I was extremely thirsty. For some reason, I had murder on my mind.

4
A HAIR'S BREADTH AWAY

May 26, 2020

I t was early morning, and the streetlights evaded the black-out drapes stealing darkness from her bedroom. Brynn rolled over and snatched the magenta blanket over her face. The clock read 4:36 AM. She slammed her head into the pillow. *I don't have to be at the shelter until 6:00 AM. I can get thirty more minutes of sleep. Where's Marc? He probably fell asleep on the couch again. Good, that leaves me more room to spread out. Damn it, stop thinking. I wonder what it feels like outside today? I hope it's not too hot. The guys suffer when it's too hot.*

One snowy Christmas Eve, when it was less than nine degrees out, Brynn wished that she could help every man left alone on the streets. She dreamt that she'd invited them into her grandmother's living room and given them big bowls of home-cooked Brunswick stew. They would each get a sleeping bag and a pillow. Even though they still had to sleep on the floor, they would have shelter, warmth, and love. They wouldn't have to worry about their things being stolen as they slept. When she woke up on Christmas Day the next morning and ran down the stairs to see that it wasn't real, she was heartbroken. From that day forward, she vowed to help. Men have a special place in her heart. She sees a bit of her dad in them. The hurt in their eyes, as if their souls need soothing. There, there, now. Her earliest memory of this pain was in her father's eyes, the day her mother died.

That morning, she woke up to the smell of bacon. It wasn't often that they bought pork because her mother said swine was unclean. So, when she let them eat it every now and then, it was the precursor to a good day. Brynn walked into the kitchen with her nose in the air, floating in the aroma. Her mother was mixing eggs and milk in a bowl on the island. Her dad was at the stove flipping pancakes. He turned around, smizing with those butterscotch brown eyes. They squinched, glimmering with happiness. He held his hand in the air for a celebratory bacon high-five, "Good morning, chipmunk." Later, that evening, he'd come home a little after Brynn, when she was standing in the doorway with blood on her bubblegum pink shirt, facing in. He stood behind her, peering over her head, his briefcase in one hand and his keys in the other. He wouldn't move. He couldn't move. All he did was stand there, staring at the love of his life, laying there, dead. Brynn turned to him. He looked at her with tormented eyes, seething, writhing with pain. She doesn't remember many things from that day, but she remembered that look. She wanted to fix it. She wanted to mend him. She wanted to do anything to make him stay. The kind of loss they experienced that day changes the pith of the mind, and it undoubtedly changed theirs. That was the last day Brynn saw her father. Even in his absence, she loves him still, but she doesn't like to think about that day. I guess the memory was scarring, I assume she repressed it. She's a trip, but I don't blame her. If I'm honest, parts of it were fuzzy for me as well. When I think back, it's as if we had been drugged, because everything looked blurry, psychedelic even.

Damn it, I guess I'm up. Brynn threw the cover off of herself and got ready to go volunteer. The early-morning mist hovered over Spring Street. It was difficult to see the path before you, no less the cars. The building was half-covered in fog, but we've been here many times. It was two stories made of old brick: reds, browns, earth tones, and pink. The parking lot was in the front and rounded, so you could go in one way and out the other. Downtown Atlanta is the home of the homeless. Nearby, a plethora of tents served as a refuge for the men that the shelter didn't have space for. Inside of the 285-perimeter, you could find these tents, grouped into little villages. At night the tents vibrated, sending heat up through the concrete, the door-flap-shaped mouths sealed shut, keeping the sleepers inside of it warm. They're an eye-sore for tourists, and the city doesn't like it. The parking lot was full of old fast-food containers and potholes, much like the rest of the city. The smell of pee was nose-burning. Next to the shelter's entrance, a man slept hunched against a brick wall with bloodstains on his shirt. His clothes were dingy and holey, over-worn and oversized. His shoes had flaps and his grayish hair was matted, it was the texture of wool. Like many times before, he had missed the cut-off time for getting into the shelter the night before, so he wasn't allowed in. Brynn bent down next to him.

"Hey, hey," she said calmly, not to alarm him.

"Huh, what?" He looked around, confused and alarmed. "Leave me alone."

"James, is your hand hurt? Let me see." She didn't bother asking what happened, she knew the nighttime could be rough. She was gentle with him. Her large, round eyes and high cheekbones smile at you even when she doesn't.

"Oh, Brynn! It's you." He sat up, untying a blood-soaked shirt from around the open gash near his thumb muscle. "Shit, it stings."

"I can help." She grabbed his hand, holding it palm up while pretending the stench of liquor and urine didn't bother her. I wrapped my strands around his hand to heal him. He was unaware of my presence, so he jerked and snatched his hand back in fear. "Your hair!" Brynn gently pulled his hand toward her again and he let her. I continued, wrapping around his hand like a self-closing bandage, pulsating until his wound went from a deep cut to a laceration.

The sign on the building read "Gintz Homeless Men's Shelter." They offer hot meals, a safe place to sleep, and limited medical care, like first aid.

Brynn told him. "You're going to have to let the nurse inside clean it and get you a bandage, so this can heal completely." For some reason, I couldn't fully heal a wound. I could stop the bleeding. I could heal the fat and sometimes the muscle, but I could never close the wound and finish the process. Still, James' eyes lit up like a seven-year-old on his first visit to Disney World.

"Thank you so much. I could have died from that wound." She smiled. Fixing him made her day.

"Can you use that good hand to help me get this food out of the trunk?"

"Yes, ma'am. Your wish is my command." He snapped to a cheaply done salute. In his eyes, she could see tears falling against a brick wall of anguish. She could see a marred soul, a bruised ego, and withering valor.

"Thanks, James. Do you think the guys will mind cheese grits again today?"

"Come on now. You know beggars can't be choosers."

"Don't say that. Being on hard times doesn't make you a beggar."

Together they carried the grocery bags inside. Before they got to the kitchen, she stopped and told him, "Drop that stuff on the counter. I'll come back for it." She motioned with her head toward a set of doors labeled Men's Showers. "When you're done, I'll see you in the cafeteria."

The soup kitchen was square-shaped with an open concept. Pans hung from the pot rack at the center. A small group of sundry volunteers in timeworn aprons prepared breakfast. The smell of sausage and coffee reminded Brynn of her grandma's house, and the weather forecast played on a loop on the TV.

"It's expected to be in the 80s this week, with a high chance of rain at the end of the week." In the corner of the screen, it read, 6:15 AM, 26 May 2020. Brynn greeted the other volunteers, a couple of whom were there as community service.

"Good morning, everyone."

Sheila responded cheerfully. "Good morning, sweetie."

"It's morning, but it ain't good." Joe declared.

Joe was the misanthropic old head. He assumed the worst in everyone. He thought the Bible was a comic book. He overused the term 'young blood' and thought 'the man' was out to get him. Maybe he was right.

"Who died?" Brynn asked jokingly in response to his negative demeanor.

Nobody laughed.

"You haven't heard the news? A Black man was murdered last night."

Brynn gaped. Goosebumps appeared on her skin. "What? Murdered? How?"

"The police, man. Same shit, different day." He shook his head, cutting onions on the stainless-steel prep table. "You're not surprised. They stay killing us."

"Okay, but what happened? How did he die? I assume he was shot?"

Joe pointed to the TV with his meat cleaver, not looking up from the onions. The news anchor spoke.

"Special Report. Tensions are high in Minneapolis after a Black man was killed by a police officer last night. He had been pinned to the ground and died. The incident was caught on camera. We will share the video, but I must warn you that the images are disturbing. We'll keep you updated as additional information is made available."

Killed? It looked to me like they misspelled murdered. The video was hard to watch and it was even harder to describe.

"I can't watch anymore. How many times have y'all seen this replay?" Brynn threw her hands up and grabbed the remote. "I can't do this. I don't want to hear it. I don't want to see it." Even though she was always trying to help someone, Brynn didn't like to see anyone suffer. She preferred to ignore it, especially if she thought she couldn't do anything to help. She ignored red flags, changed channels, and disregarded the truth. She distracted herself. She wanted it out of her mind so she could keep sporting those rose-colored glasses with a smile on her face.

"You better not change that channel, missy," Joe commanded, still not looking up from the onions.

"Calm down, baby, ain't nothing we can do." Sheila patted Brynn's upper arm.

Brynn responded, "Maybe we should try? Aren't you tired of this, Ms. Sheila?"

"Let's do what we came here to do. Let's help the men at this shelter eat. They are still alive." Sheila turned to Brynn. "I already have a big pot filled with water on the stove for them grits that I know you brought."

Sheila is the nonpartisan negro. She was partial to herself, preferring to get the work done and go home. Never fighting back and never speaking up. A younger guy had his back to the three of them, not saying a word. This was his first time volunteering at the shelter. He was flipping sausages, slapping them back down with fury. Brynn meandered to the stove next to him, dragging her feet because she felt guilty for not being able to help, but she thought Sheila was right. Confounded, she increased the heat on the gas stove and fixated on the flames, they were reaching out in the shape of hands and long limbs, trying to grasp something to set afire, so she turned the burner down slightly and the hands slid back down. She stared, imagining that officer rolling around, jerking about, burning in the flames. She wondered, *who's next? Will I see Marc on the TV, Cory, my dad? Would I even recognize my dad if I saw him? They'll probably kill me, too, once they learn I have powers.* She grabbed a measuring glass and the grits, pulled in her lips, and held back the tears.

"We're back with more information." The news anchor returned. "Four officers have been fired for the death of a Black man, who was handcuffed, pinned to the ground for almost ten minutes, and pleading for help. He was heard saying that he couldn't breathe numerous times."

The new guy had been silently enraged, boiling, ready to bubble up. He turned away from the sausages, yelling at the TV. "Ten minutes? Ten-fucking-minutes. Accidents happen or whatever. But this ain't that. This cop had ten minutes to think about what he was doing, yet he still did it. That's murder! When is this going to stop?"

Joe responded with disdain, "Wake up, young blood. It's not."

"Well, what are we going to do about it?" Brynn asked.

Joe dropped the cleaver, irritated. He answered in despair, "Be Black and die."

I wondered when Brynn would wake up to reality and stop pretending. But honestly, one doesn't just wake up. You don't jump out the bed in the morning, *on-go*. We wake up gradually and intentionally. Otherwise, we fall back to sleep. We've all had that moment. You fought it, but it was time to wake up. That moment a person said or did some shit so fucked up, you could feel the heat radiating from your insides, and you could feel the lava spewing out of your ears. Your heart rate increased, and your hands started to shake. You probably thought to yourself: Today is the day blue eyes die. Waking up came with growing up. Growing came with aging, and who wants that because aging means death, right? Her words, not mine. I died all the time. I grew. I died. Everyday. But you have to die to be born again. You have to be born to live. Admitting the truth will make her hate them the way I hate them. It will make her hate herself for not living up to what everyone wanted her to be. Or so she thought. In the meantime, she preferred to feign happiness, but her smile is painted on... Like a clown, minus the bab-ass wig because I'm a badass bitch. For me, it was when this white woman put her hands on us at the park. I'll get to that soon. For Brynn, well, she took more time than the rest of us. Don't forget, she had a heart of rose gold and a pair of rose-colored glasses to match. In her defense, she's an empath. She felt everything, but seeing the world for what it was would take her down a spiral. Her whole world would be flipped upside down, and I didn't know if she could take it. The bed was a safe place. Lay there long enough, and it felt like a self-regulated heater, keeping the warmth in. The comfort keeps you stuck. The mattress pulls you in, sinking just enough that it feels like you left the stress of life but not so much that you feel like you can't *get out*. Your body left an indenture. Sometimes, you wake up with a yelp because it feels like there's nothing beneath you. You're falling into the abyss, paralyzed. Don't worry. Go back to sleep. Relax. Your dreams will keep you safe. I lied. They won't. Today, Brynn began to wake up.

5
WELL-GROOMED

May 27, 2020

Brynn needed a breather and a pause in life. So, when Marc didn't pick up the phone, she called Cory to take her to her favorite park. He picked her up in a 1986 tan box Chevy Caprice that his dad left him before he died. They built that car from the ground up, putting love and care into every detail. Sitting in Cory's car, Brynn felt understood. When she needed a shoulder to cry on, his was a sponge. He turned down the music and said, "You know I'm supposed to be at the gym?" She smirked and gave him the side eye because she knew the gym wasn't more important than her.

"Don't worry," she said, "your little girlfriends will be at the gym tomorrow." He laughed, and she turned in his direction, waiting for his smile. He had one dimple on his right cheek. How lucky for the passenger. They met in middle school, in gym class. He was tall for his age, strong too. He mastered and finished all of the physical activities before everyone else. After putting forth only the effort needed to pass the class, Brynn would sit at the top of the bleachers and wait. Like clockwork, minutes later, he joined. They talked about everything and went in on everybody.

Almost every weekend, they gamed at his house. She didn't consider herself a nerd until she met him. She had a Nintendo pre-Cory, but could only remember playing Duck Hunt and Tetris. He got her into first-person shooter games. Every year on release day, they stood in line at GameStop for the new video game drops. That was until she met Marc, who didn't like video games, and definitely didn't like Cory. Cory used to rock a little curly afro fade with short sides. These days, he kept it faded with a fresh lineup and waves. But it's the mustache and beard for me. He's an eyebrow slit away from being a pretty boy.

Speaking of slits. When he bit his bottom lip, and that soul patch stood up, Brynn got insta-wet. The man was a perfect specimen. She was crushing on Cory, but she wouldn't act on it because she didn't want to ruin their friendship, and she didn't think he had feelings for her. Maybe in the next lifetime. Now that he was older, he gave linebacker vibes, like could hold his own in a fight. He dressed well and never sagged. That day, he wore gray Nike sweatpants with a white crew-neck tee that hugged his muscles.

They headed northeast on Memorial Drive. Brynn focused her attention on the stained, worn-out mattress on the side of the road. It was melting above the heat of the asphalt streets, and the springs were desperately trying to get out. *Who the hell dumps a whole-ass mattress?* She heard police sirens approaching from the rear. As the patrol car passed them on the right, Brynn fixated on the blue lights. She was thrown back into the feeling that she was trying to escape. Whenever something happened to someone in the news, Brynn thought of how it could have been her or someone she knew. Her mind wandered. She felt their pain, grieved their loss, and shed their tears. She played the footage in her mind over and over. She wished she could pretend it didn't happen like everyone else. The recent news bothered her more than usual because this victim didn't get shot like the others. She convinced herself that the others died faster when they'd been shot. She told herself that their life didn't flash before them because they didn't have the time, they couldn't regret being in the wrong place at the wrong time because everything happened so fast. They couldn't hope to say goodbye because they were taking their last breath. They didn't feel any pain: That's what she made herself believe. It helped her sleep at night.

This time, she knew that wasn't the case. She knew exactly how long it took. Nine minutes and twenty-nine seconds. This time she knew that he cried out. She heard him do it. She heard him say his goodbyes. "Tell my kids I love them," he said. She heard him cry out for his mother, and that's worse than having to say goodbye to your children. He became as helpless and vulnerable as a child himself. That's what hurt. No one wanted to see a child suffer, he needed protection and he needed love. He got neither. It's like his inner child is suffering in a forever loop. She could only be glad his mother wasn't alive to witness her baby boy being murdered. This affected Brynn, but she got so wrapped up in the emotions that she became paralyzed. She couldn't do anything because she wanted to do everything. She wanted revenge. She wanted to travel back in time, but mostly she wanted a better Amerikkka.

Brynn had been thinking for a while when Cory looked over at her, worried. He laid his hand on hers, then moved it after a few seconds. "You're quiet today. What's up witcha?" She was normally so silly and animated around him.

She held her right hand out before her, pretending to look at her nails. "You know, same ole, same ole."

He tilted his head sideways, giving her a quick side-eye because he knew there was something wrong, but she didn't like talking about things. He looked at her again. "Are you going to tell me, or do I have to take you to my mom's for some cookies and therapy? She'll get it up out ya, but you won't like it."

Brynn loved Mrs. Williams. She was the next best thing to grandma. When Brynn was younger, they would sit at the kitchen table and talk. His mom never judged. When Brynn had a rough day and didn't want to open up, his mom would coerce it out of her with some right-out-the-oven caramel pecan chocolate chip cookies and milk. She always knew how to comfort her. Brynn looked at the car's roof, hoping sheer will would hold back the tears.

"I'm just tired. I hate hearing about police murdering Black men. I wish they would stop. I wish I could make it stop. No matter what we do, vote, protest, or ask nicely, they don't stop. I don't know why this is bothering me this much. It's not like my crying is going to change anything. It feels like a downhill battle."

"There's always something. You need that push, that motivation."

"What do you mean push? I'm motivated. I use my motivation to help the folks that need my help. I volunteer to help the homeless, hungry, and in need."

"That's a good start. I'm not saying you need to do anything differently, but if it's bothering you this much, then write a book or become a politician. Shit, I don't know. Find out where the racists live and scrap." He chuckled to lighten the mood.

"I guess," she said despondently, changing the subject. "When was the last time we were here, at the park?"

"A couple of years ago. It was before you got with that clown ass nigga." She didn't respond, the same way he didn't respond when she brought up his little girlfriends at the gym.

"That's right, give him the same energy, boo." I was all for that, just like a best friend would be.

Brynn became animated, gesturing with her hands at every word. "Remember when we tried to feed the ducks that day, but some geese came out of nowhere chasing us?"

"Hell yeh. They came out the bushes like 'dis a stickup, gimme all your bread.'" He held his hand like a gun, pointing it at the windshield. They both giggled.

"Right, then I dropped some and they started fighting over it. The ducks got the hell out of the way. I never knew geese were so aggressive."

6
UNRULY

May 27, 2020

Southern Peaks Park has an immoral past. One unaligned with freedom and the future that Black people seek. It celebrates the resistance to desegregation and the Ku Klux Klan's role in its foundation. There are old slave cabins that thrive on the property. Originally, the structures were moved in from old plantations for the taping of a popular historic romance film but remained thereafter. Now, they serve as historic monuments for parkgoers. An *attraction*, they call it. The park is packed with memorials to the Confederacy. Their flags flapped in the wind. Going there is like saying: I'm fine with the past, I'm fine with how they treat us, I'm fine with their stubbornness to change. It's okay. I'm fine. Albeit Atlanta being dubbed the "City in the Forest," most of it is just buildings, traffic, and dirt. It's not the greenery one would hope for with that nickname but that's why Brynn loves to visit Southern Peaks. The grass is green, the trees wave, and the trails are plentiful. Here, she gets a sip of nature and an intermission of life. She wouldn't tell her friends that this is her sanctuary. They wouldn't call her double-standard, hypocritical, and phony to her face, but they would think it. For most people born around Atlanta, this 1,700-foot mountain is the largest one they'll ever see in person. Standing on the vast green lawn in front of it, you could plainly see the godawful bas-relief of three men on horses that represented this place. It was equivalent to three acres in size, more extensive than a football field. The message was blatant. You couldn't miss it if you tried. She loved the park, but she wasn't blind.

Cory pulled through the main entry plaza and the woman pushed open a sliding glass window to hand Cory their ticket. Going to the park was a mental reset for Brynn. Most folks would say they want to get out in nature to be alone, go hunting, fishing, or run. They'd say they want to enjoy the calm and quiet. If she went somewhere absent of people, it made her feel empty. She preferred to be around others, but not in conversation with them, that was too draining. She was good with a friendly nod from a stranger jogging by. She loved the sound of people chattering and toddlers giggling at simple things, like leaves falling. If not for bugs and animals, she could live outside in this very park. The Memorial Lawn was a huge area of grass that lay before the mountain. On each side of the lawn, there are a total of thirteen terraces dedicated to the states that seceded. Each has a corresponding state flag and informational displays that tell of their history during the Civil War. Standing in the middle of the lawn, Brynn closed her eyes and took a deep breath.

"Listen, you smell that, Cory? They just cut the grass today, and I swear I can still hear the lawnmower. Maybe it's just my imagination. Take a puff of that green," she chuckled. The blades of grass vibrated in the cool wind.

He looked around, noticing a man in the distance wearing a red hat with words written in white letters. He couldn't be sure, but he assumed it was the symbol of hate he was so unfond of. He stepped closer to Brynn and crossed his arms, keeping his head on the swivel. "You love this park, huh?" He asked.

"Yeh, nature is intoxicating."

She let the sun bite her neck, and when it started to sting, she made her way to a shaded walking path. Brist Mill on the Chickasaw Trail is her go-to. The park is 3200 acres of huge, so you can't get to one location without passing something else first. On the way was Lake Frontage, she couldn't help but stop. It was one of her favorite spots there.

"Let's feed the ducks for old-time sake. I brought some bread."

He looked at her quizzically with a half-smile. "And get attacked by geese again? I'm straight."

Water bumped lightly against the rocks and the little ducks floated on the ripples, moving with the waves. There was always a pack of them, and sometimes a handful of geese, huddled up near a raised geomorphic embankment that flanked the lake. A broad oak tree stood tall, seemingly growing out of the embankment. It was breathtaking, invigorating, like something from a fairy tale. The only thing Brynn didn't care for was the building that sat unused, becoming more of an eyesore each day. It used to be an attraction that used amphibious vehicles, which were referred to as Ducks. They called it Duck Sails. They no longer operated but the structure remained. The real ducks stayed in this one particular spot, even though the lake stretched over 300 acres. I assumed that this was because of people, like Brynn, who liked to feed them, even though there was a sign that read, "DON'T FEED THE DUCKS."

Brynn's phone dinged. It was a text from Marc. *Oh, now he can reply.* She clicked the side button and stuck it in her back pocket. As they threw bread at the ground, the geese bullied their way through the ducks, taking bread for themselves, leaving the ducks with crumbs. The saliva slung from their ravenous mouths and they clucked aggressively. They fought with each other like it was life or death, and they weren't afraid of humans. Geese never change. Since they were so riled up, it was probably a good time to leave, but Brynn noticed a duckling hiding in the bushes.

"I wonder why this one isn't eating," she said.

"Maybe it's full."

"I think something's wrong with it."

"How about we stay in our lane and let nature take care of it."

"If you were hurt, wouldn't you want someone to help you?"

Brynn stepped into the muddy water and reached through the bush, getting scratched by the branches that felt dry and hot. A thousand eyes inside the bark blinked as she pushed them to the side. "It'll be all right. I'm here to help."

The duck chirped, crying out of fear, but no other duck came to save it. Brynn cupped it in her hand, and I gently hugged its brown and yellow feathery body. The duckling started to perk up and flap its wings, jumping out of her hand into the lake's edge, near a big oak tree.

"Much better. No harm in lending a helping hand." She looked at Cory as if to say *I told you so.*

Cory shrugged and smiled. Across the lake, melodramatic melodies chimed like the middle of a creepy movie when the killer lurks behind a tree. It was coming from a spiraling, industrial-looking structure made of redwood and steel. It stood thirteen stories high with about a hundred speakers that play instrumentals from a carillon, with over 700 hundred bells. Various songs were remade from genres such as Goth, Flemish, and Baroque-European associations. Reminiscent of church bells, its purpose was to invoke a feeling of goodwill and harmony. To me, it sounded like a clarinet and an organ having breakup sex, like something the Germans play before exterminating the Jews, the calm before a sinking ship. Brynn ignored that too. Her phone dinged again. She ignored it again, looking at the oak tree. Her eyes lit up, and so did the oaks.

"Let's carve our names in this tree. That'd be cute."

He laughed, "You corny, but I don't have a knife."

"I have an idea." She gets closer to the oak tree. "This one should do."

I'd never done it before, but I took the shape of a sword tip and carved their names in the tree. "Look, it's working," she said, surprised and excited.

"Bet. Do yo' thang."

I cut through the bark and felt it shudder, etching at it until it said, "Cory & Brynn BFF's forever."

If I had eyes, they would've been rolling on the ground. I wished they would've stopped playing with each other and went on a date. "Get a room," I said but it was like talking to that big ass tree.

"What do you think?" she asked.

"It's straight or whatever," he smirked, his dimple smiling back at Brynn. "Is there a bathroom around here somewhere, maybe by the exit?"

"It's one by the trail where we were headed. Come on."

They walked back to the street toward Brist Mill, traveling down the sidewalk laced with trees. On the other side of the street, a picnic area studded with grills and bench tables sat empty. They're usually jam-packed during the 4th of July or some major barbecuing type of holiday. People on bikes whizzed by, leaving a slight wind against Brynn's arm. She watched as they disappeared over the hilly road where they were headed.

"You see that?" Cory said with discomposure. "I guess they're rallying today." He signaled in the direction of a grey-haired man sitting at the corner of an intersection, in his Confederate lawn chair with his Confederate shirt and coffee mug. They liked to go all out.

"I don't give them the time of day. Just ignore him." Brynn said.

"I can't. He's just sitting here like it's all good."

"Is it not?" Brynn questioned.

"What do you mean?"

"Is it not all good for them? I mean, he's white with a Confederate flag. This is their space. The carving of three men on the side of the mountain, they don't call it the Confederate Memorial Carving for nothing."

"Bet. So, you 'bout ready to get up outta here then?"

"Nah. You said you needed to use the bathroom. Plus, they're not going to do anything. They mind their business. We mind ours."

He looked at her in disbelief. Most Black people who visit Southern Peaks Park are alike in that they take the good with the bad. Everyday ain't birds singing and sun-shining at the park. Rarely when we're here, but likely regularly for themselves, the Confederates show up. They come in droves with four Confederate flags on each corner of their car. Flags on their shirts, hats, chairs, shoes, you name it. They hold flags. It's asinine the number of flags they have. They roll down their window and stare blankly, like robots. The Confederates have been told to stop coming by whoever owns the park, but they do what they want. I mean, who is going to stop them? Who is going to police the police?

When they reached the bathrooms, Brynn sat on a nearby bench taking in the pink flowers and the happy faces inside of them. Not even a minute into daydreaming, she felt a tug at her hair. A shriek came from behind before she could turn around, and a woman with a nasal voice hollered, "What in tarnation!" The woman stood there with her cadaverous face all shriveled up, and the creases around her mouth wrinkled. Her wrinkles had wrinkles. She held her hand close to her chest like we had taken something from her.

"Your hair bit me!" Wow! The nerve of this woman. The flagrant moxie! Say it with me. Never touch a Black woman's hair. That's law.

Brynn felt something warm drip on her nape. She knew what it was, but denied the truth. "You're crazy!"

Screaming in a Southern drawl, articulating to her best, but falling short, the woman said, "How dare you tell me what I just felt?"

My sudden reaction to bite her was the reflex of my ancestors. The blood trickled down my tips and into my cuticle. Her pain, my pleasure. My only regret was not slapping her too.

"Stop yelling. I can help you. Let me see it." Brynn reached out.

"No! Don't come closer."

I couldn't believe Brynn wanted to heal this mouth breather. Hurriedly, I stretched out toward her wound. Could you imagine someone's hair growing twelve inches right before your eyes? The woman gasped and tried to pull her arm back, but I snatched it back in. "Oh now, you want to keep your hands to yourself?" I wrapped myself around the woman's hand and in an instant, she was healed.

"You're one of them, aren't you?" Her volume increased again, and people started to look on, "She's one of them. She's one of them!"

"Oh my god, you don't have to be so loud."

People started to murmur and get closer. As more park-goers looked on, Brynn searched for an escape route but noticed a group of men staring from a short distance. They leaned pompously against a white lifted truck with floodlights and a smoke stack exhaust. A grille guard threw in for added intimidation. Confederate flags wafting prejudice in the wind. Brynn was caught in a stare-off, like a deer in headlights. She snapped out of it when Cory tapped her on the shoulder.

"Move! Get the fuck out the way!" He pushed people aside to get to her. "Come on, Brynn, let's go."

As they fled, making their way back to the car, Brynn skimmed the crowd. Her eyes dashed about as she noticed the angry pale faces and the ashamed brown ones.

"What happened?" He asked.

"That lady touched my hair."

Brynn downplayed the fuckery. That lady yanked her hair.

"I was sitting there minding my business. I guess I zoned out and was caught off guard because she was yelling about my hair biting her the next thing I knew. How does that even make sense?" Brynn was deflecting again.

"Did you?" Cory asked.

"Did I what?"

"Did you bite her?"

Brynn hadn't, but I had. How else was I to be fed?

"She was behind me. How could I have bit her?"

"Shit, you tell me," Cory said, unsettled. "You're the one with the hair-bili-ties. Maybe, you got emotional and cut her?"

He was right. *I* did get emotional, but I was validated.

"Why would I do that?" Brynn asked.

They were interrupted by the increasing sound of exhaust from an engine revving. It got louder and louder until it was upon them. They turned around to see a white truck hurtling toward them. Cory yelled, "Fuck! Move!" They bolted, running up the sidewalk, but the truck advanced. The driver stuck his head out the window, "You can't outrun this, Hemi, scum monkeys." The truck jumped the sidewalk and sped up, "I ain't letting y'all get out of here alive, so you might as well stop trying." I was like, let me stop you right there. I don't play that shit. I got big on his ass. He only saw a bunch of hair pushing against his truck's grill. I slowed it enough to startle the driver to a halt.

"What in the unholy hell? Get your goddamn demonic hands off my truck."

The door opened, and I wrapped around his legs and arms, slamming him to the ground face-first. With a mouth full of pavement, all he could do was holler. Now that he was disarmed of his vehicular arms, Cory and Brynn kept running until they reached the car. Her phone dinged. She opened the passenger door, panting.

"That was them. The dudes that were staring at me when you were in the bathroom."

"They saw what you did?"

"They were too far to see anything."

"Too far. That's not good enough, Brynn."

"It's all I got. Let's go."

May 27, 2020

The sky was a morose peach. The alter ego of dawn was looming, and the lady in the glass ticket box had closed up shop. Brynn sat up and looked out the car window, "What the hell is going on?"

Cory motioned to a crowd, as they drove closer. "You see what I see?"

"The Confederate flags, the people, the line of cars? I see a lot."

"That's 12."

"Great, maybe they have it under control." She was naïve in that way, always hoping for the best in people.

"They got it under control, all right," he replied mockingly.

Brynn closed her eyes, looking down and shaking her head, "I don't feel like dealing with this."

What seemed like a bullet dodged became another one in the chamber. Brynn and Cory heard yelling as they approached the main exit gate. Amongst the swarm, people were trying to leave, and a mob was there to stop them. I didn't wake up and choose violence... But it chose me. Brynn's eyes opened wide, and she squinted, "It can't be."

"What?"

"How did he get up here so fast?"

"Hemi, it gives you wings," I joked to myself.

She took a deep breath, noticing the white truck from earlier blocking an exit lane. His comrades blocked the others. Cory came to a stop. They exited the car with little movement as if it would make them invisible. They entered the conversation in the middle of the madness. A middle-aged schmuck donning a red cowboy hat with white stars in the shape of a blue X stood in the middle of the exit lane. He yelled, "I'll say it again. Y'all can leave when we get the girl." Behind each word he spoke, I could hear a banjo playing country music. People were shouting,

"We don't know what you're talking about."..."Let us leave." ..."Move."

"Figure it out." He pointed at random people. "That scuzzy needs to pay."

A bald man furrowed his brow. "What scuzzy? What girl? What is going on?"

"One of them Blacks, a root-witch. Now, don't make me get ugly. We're just going to sit and wait until one of you's finds her."

The bald man looked at one of the assailants holding a tire iron and another with a pistol. "Why the weapons?"

"For our protection," the man with the cowboy hat replied.

"Did I hear him right, his protection?" He looked left at a Black woman next to him and repeated the word sarcastically, "A tire iron and a gun are for his protection?" He scoffed brazenly, throwing a dismissive hand toward the men. Then he looked over at a cop standing nearby,

"You ain't going to do anything about this?"

Arms crossed, the cop responded, "I'm off-duty."

"You're allowed to be in uniform off-duty?"

The cop looked the man in his eyes, then down at his shoes, and then back into his eyes. The condescending body language of the cop drew Brynn's attention. She couldn't help but notice his eyes. One green and one grey. They reminded her of a dog she once had, destructive, but an excellent watchdog. Border collie, purebred.

"Purebred? More like inbred." I cracked myself up.

Brynn met eyes with the driver of the truck as he stepped back out with a baseball bat, swinging it in the air with a smirk, not losing eye contact, not even to blink. His nose and chin were scratched and tinged with blood from the face plant. I could've devoured him right there. The adrenaline must've gotten to his head because he pointed at Brynn with the bat.

"There she is."

Brynn and Cory snatched their heads toward each other. Without words, they were instantly on the same page. Cory's door slammed shut, but someone grabbed Brynn by her shoulders and lifted her a few inches off the ground. She flailed and kicked.

"Let me go. Let me go."

Cory leaned into the passenger seat, trying to grab her legs and pull her in.

"Bruh, what the fuck! Get the fuck back," he shouted at the man.

Now, I had to be the bad guy. "Unhand her, you uncouth rat. She didn't give you enthusiastic consent." I lifted his fingers off of her shoulder and stretched them all backward toward his arm. At the same time, I grabbed the wrist on his other arm, pulsating energy into him, altering his mood and his morality so that he could actually feel remorse. He calmed down, and let go because anger was no longer palpitating through his psyche. Brynn leaped into the passenger seat, locking the doors immediately.

"We had her. Why'd you let go?" The schmuck yelled.

His wife parroted him. "Yeh, why'd you let go?"

The uncouth rat looked down at his hands. He responded but they couldn't hear him. "I don't know. Something came over me. I just... It didn't feel right."

Cory put the car in reverse, tapping a van behind them. That wasn't there before.

"You ain't leaving without saying bye, are ya?" Someone shouted from the mob.

"Fuck, Fuck, Fuck! What do you want? Just let us go," Brynn cried.

"You need to pay."

"Pay for what, psycho?"

"You know what you did. My wife says you hurt her."

"She hurt me! I helped her." Brynn cried.

His wife spoke, "You helped me after you bit me... You and yer damn demon hair."

"I don't want to fight. Just let us go."

"If you don't pay, then someone else will. I know how you root-witches are. You think you can do whatever you want and not deal with the consequences."

I had never seen nor heard of another like us. Now, all of a sudden, he knew all about us. He even had a name made up for us. Where is this coming from?

Brynn instructed Cory, "When I say so, hit the gas."

I stretched my tresses, growing about twenty feet in length. The schmuck kept yelling,

"You ain't helping the situation. You're just causing more problems, getting in the way."

I was outstretched, sitting on Brynn's lap like a massive ball of yarn—pieces of me were twirling and twisting, dancing. I was excited to show out. Brynn rolled the window down, and I slipped out, sliding down the side of the car like a python on the hunt, ready for action. Brynn yelled,

"NOW! Go, Go, Go!" Cory stomped on the gas, and their heads jerked backward into the headrests. Someone shoved a bystander in front of the car, forcing their hand, but destiny was about to have a three-way because we couldn't stop in time. Frozen, unable to scream in fear or remove herself, the bystander gaped, stuck on all fours. I thrust her to the side, tossing her out of the way. The car missed her by a hairsbreadth. Brynn and Cory's heads jerked forward when the car stopped. Onlookers mumbled, and the mob was vindicated. Brynn had proven that she is, in fact, a root-witch. Everyone saw her power. There's no hiding who we are now. They know. I said it before and I'll say it again, I couldn't hide who I was if I tried. Murmurs ensued,

"What was that? Did you see that? Maybe she will save us. Free us so that we can go home."

Schmuck shook his head, "Now see, I knew it. You can't help yourself. The savage is strong in this one." He reached for a shotgun in his backseat.

Like a tidal wave in the ocean, I rose, towering over him. Swaying, my jet-black silky mane proved menacing, he stood there with his mouth hanging open. "Make a move, buddy. It's just you and me." He may not have heard me, but my intent was apparent. "You've got about five seconds... 3, 2, 1."

"I ain't a-scared of a little—"

Before he could finish, his body thwacked against the car door and he fell like a dirty rag after a mud shower. I noticed blood from his nose, and a sense of déjà vu overcame me. This was going to be delectable. I slathered it all over me. I absorbed the essence. I could breathe. As I relaxed, contracting back to size, Brynn frantically hauled me back into the car as we left. We could stop looking over their shoulders and focus on the orange sky west because the darkness was behind us. That's what I thought, anyway. Brynn's phone rang. She silenced it and unraveled the plastic from a piece of candy. A Lemonhead.

"That took a lot out of me," she said wearily. "I'm tired." Of course, she was. She's not a superhero. She's not really here to save the world. Besides, she always falls out when I overexert. Getting big on that dude was too much. Changing lengths multiple times didn't help. Cory felt bad for her. He suggested food to get her energy back.

"Let's stop and get you something to eat."

"I got food at home," she replied sleepily.

"Either someone's following us, or their headlights are broken." Cory looked at the rearview mirror, squinting his eyes. He looked uneasy.

Brynn's head plopped against the window. "We gotta slay low."

Cory scrunched his eyebrows. "Huh?"

"I said... Let's... Lay..." The candy rolled out of Brynn's mouth and onto the floor as we fell asleep.

8
KERATINIZATION

Jacqori - May 27, 2020

"**B**rynn, Wake up!"

She mumbled inaudibly, not waking from my yells.

"Brynn... Brynn," I nudged her, but nothing.

I tried to distract myself with best-case scenario of who might be in the car behind us. I bet her dude is about to be at her crib waiting again like the mark ass nigga he is. Hell, that's probably him behind us now. Stalker. He can't show up for a date but will show up to mark his territory. He doesn't deserve her. He doesn't appreciate her the way I do. Like the day she wanted to climb up that big tree in her yard. We were young, she loved climbing trees back then. Always been a lover of nature. She went up first like it was nothing. Climbing trees wasn't really my thing, but I tried anyway... For her. I almost made it up there before I slipped. I tried to catch my fall by jumping and ended up twisting my ankle. She rushed down to me, knelt before my leg, and her damn hair slid around my ankle so fast that I thought I was seeing things, but she was healing me. The throbbing in my ankle stopped, but it navigated up to my heart. She was so gentle with me. I felt taken care of. I stood to my feet and held my hands out. Her eyes glazed over in admiration and her smile sang to me. She smelled as sweet as jasmine, familiar, like something I always wanted nearby. Her skin, her hair, everything about her is soft. Even her hugs nourish me.

I was still paranoid about the unmarked car behind me, so I turned down the music to concentrate.

"Damn, I know objects are closer than they appear, but I ain't crazy. This person definitely sped up."

The car turned on its bright lights and the beam through the window made it difficult to see.

"Here we go with this bullshit. I guess now your lights work. He probably thinks he scaring somebody on that creep shit. I can't wait to see what this shit is about."

I hit the brakes and Brynn's head bobbed forward, but she didn't wake up. I reached out to catch her, pushing her head back into a comfortable position. That's when I heard a screeching sound from behind. The car tires skidded and the brakes squeaked. Their car door slammed shut. I hopped out of the car 38-hot,

"Man, what's your problem?"

The light was blinding, but the silhouette of a man marched toward me with anger in his stride.

"Yo man, why are you following us?" I could barely make out what looked like a gun pointing my way.

A booming voice yelled from the light, "Get on the ground!"

I noticed a blue suit and an obscured badge. I hesitantly put my hands in the air.

"For what? I didn't do anything wrong."

"Because I said so. Get down on the ground, now."

"Sir, I think you got the wrong dude. I just left the park, and I'm just trying to get home with my lady friend here."

"Are you disobeying orders, boy? I'm not going to tell you again."

"Boy? Really?" I reluctantly got down one knee at a time, hands still in the air.

"Give me your license and don't move. Why were you driving like a damn idiot?"

"Why are you following folks with your headlights off? I thought you were someone 'bout to rob us."

"That's not what I asked you, son. That's you people that like robbing," the cop insisted.

"First off, I'm not ya' son. Second, what you know about my people?"

"You got a smart mouth, don't you? Stay right here. And keep your hands up." The cop reupholstered his gun.

On my knees next to the open car door, I can see Brynn still asleep. *Damn, if I had just kept driving, this wouldn't be happening. Hopefully, she doesn't get sucked into this. He can arrest me and let her go. She got enough going on. She don't need this.*

The cop returned. "Did you know your registration was expired?"

I shook my head. "Lies. I update it every year."

"Stand up, and face the car with your hands behind your back."

Pulling me up from the ground by my shoulder and shoving me chest-first into the side of the car, the cop yanked my arms backward. I yelled, "They can't go back any more. Damn."

The cop shoved me again to make sure I couldn't move.

"What are you arresting me for? I wasn't speeding, and my registration is up to date. Y'all computer must be busted or something."

"Are you telling me how to do my job, boy?" The cop pinned me against the car, sticking his hand in my pants. Jerking away, I could feel the cop put more force into my shoulder blade.

"What you doin,' bruh? This shit right here is illegal. I hope you getting it all on camera."

Reaching around, patting my thighs, the cop asked, "You got anything on you that I should know about?"

"Only thing in my pants is my wallet and my dick. I still wanna know why you hemming me up like this?"

Growing frustrated, the cop became more aggressive with his search, almost pulling my sweatpants down. "That's not my pocket, man. You 'bout to have me assed out." I tried to turn around without further pissing off the officer.

"Stop resisting." He pushed me again. "I know you got something on you. Smart-asses like you are always hiding something." He reached around to the back of my pants, shoving his fingers between my butt cheeks.

"Bruh, what the fuck, bruh, nah." I wrestled to get free. "It's not even going down like that today."

Struggling to get his handcuffs out, the cop yelled at me. "Stop resisting and put your hands behind your fucking back."

I twisted my shoulders to the left, jerking abruptly, and made a spin move to get out of his hold. He grabbed at me but only caught air. I didn't want to fight, so I dodged, but I wasn't lucky the next time. He put every bit of his weight into tackling me to the ground, grappling my arms behind me so I couldn't cushion the fall. I hit the pavement face-first, the heat of it pulsated against my cheek and the handcuffs fell beside me. We started to scuffle. He took deep, short breaths while I held mine in suspense. It was every man for himself. We tussled and I could see the cop reaching for his gun. I caught a glimpse of Brynn, still knocked out. Time slowed down, and I wondered how this would play out. *Would I be the next victim she cried over? I'm never going to see my mom again. I didn't get a chance to say goodbye.* The thoughts kept coming. He straddled me, angling his gun.

"Where's all that smart-mouth shit now, boy?" The cop knew he had the upper hand.

"It doesn't have to be like this. I just want to go home." He said nothing, my pleas were met with silence. He coughed up a loogie and spat it on the side of my car. The fire in my eyes put a slow, sadistic smile on his face. Looking at the handcuffs on the pavement, he reached for them and turned toward my car, "What, you like that car or something?"

"You gon' arrest me now? For what? For nothing."

"I'm going to give this scrap bucket a new paint job."

"Don't touch my car, man. This shit ain't funny no more."

The cop shoved his knee into my chest and flung open the handcuffs with the single-strand point facing out. The loud scrapping pierced my ears as the cop ran the handcuffs alongside the door.

"What the fuck, man? I'ma kick yo' ass for that."

"I do believe you threatened an officer. I will add that to the charges too." He chuckled. As he continued to scrape the side of my car, I could hear Brynn rustle.

"Okay, shit, you win. Lock me up but cut that shit out."

The cop could see me staring at Brynn out of the corner of his eye. "You like her, don't you? Let me get you in these cuffs and see if she's more compliant."

I snapped, reaching up to take his gun, but it slipped from my fingers. The cop got a hold of it and pulled the trigger, I smacked the gun just in time. The bullet ricocheted elsewhere and we began to tussle again. He attempted with his gun again, aiming for my head. I looked over at Brynn. I knew this was it. I wasn't afraid to die, I knew that the minute he jumped out of the car, there was a chance that things could go sideways. The tears I shed were for the people that I didn't want to leave, the people I didn't want crying over me, the people I loved. Staring at my oldest and closest friend, my love for her hit me. I love her, I love her and I never said it. I never took the chance to see what we could have been. I never took the chance to get her away from that asshole that made her cry so damn much. I never took the chance to kiss her.

"Fighting only makes it worse!"

"I'm not going down without a fight," I exclaimed.

Putting all his weight behind the gun, he forced it closer and closer to my face. I looked deep into his eyes, glaring with disgust. His face wasn't the last thing I wanted to see before I died. I looked at Brynn one last time. My throbbing heart cried out, not being able to say goodbye. I needed nourishment. I needed to be taken care of. I needed to be embraced. I smiled. I smiled at her, remembering the way she would sing to me with her smile. I felt the gun press against my forehead. I'm tired. I can't win this. I smiled at her to say goodbye, I smiled before the shot went off and my arms dropped.

9
ACTIVATOR

May 27, 2020

Brynn came to. It took her eyes a second to adjust to the darkness, but the lightning bugs in the far-off distance offered assistance. All she could hear was the sound of chirping crickets. Looking at the Lemonhead on the floor, she realized that the recent events must've taken quite a toll.

"How long have I been asleep?" She didn't get a response. *Am I dreaming?* No, no one asks if they are dreaming in a dream. She shook off the confusion. *Where is Cory?* She looked up to see a fire truck. Exiting the car, she used her hands to block the flickering blue lights surrounding her. Police chattered amongst themselves, whispered even. Steam came up from the pavement like smoke, everything felt hot. Before she could get someone's attention, she noticed something white from the corner of her eye. It was Cory, lying there, covered in a white sheet. She refused to lift it.

"Oh my God! Please, God. Please tell me I'm dreaming. Oh my God." Her hands shook as she reached for him. "Please God, please don't be Cory."

She wanted to savor every second of uncertainty, so I pulled the sheet back for her. Brynn released a sound from the rips of her soul. It sounded like bagpipes crying. Her cry was splintered and she was wreathed in agony, twisted in folds. It was as if Leviathan reached through her guts, clawing at her insides, gnawing at her pain, causing hideous damage. I had never seen her cry like that. The sight of his wounds startled her backward. She tripped, catching herself with the palm of her hands. She got back up, kneeling beside his corpse. She leaned over him and I hugged his face to heal him. I could feel his pain and hunger for revenge. I felt death come into me and life into him. My roots felt heavy, like wet dread. Even with the hole in his face, Brynn thought she could heal him if she wanted it bad enough. She squeezed her eyes shut and grabbed the sides of his face. She gave it everything she had, but she emanated anger instead. She was furious. I was furious. She couldn't heal him, and even if she could control her emotions long enough, it still wouldn't be enough. What's dead is gone, and what's gone can't be brought back. She's in denial, and the truth hurts. A woman with small knotless ombre braids, wearing skinny jeans and a midnight blue blazer, hurriedly approached Brynn.

"Hey! You can't touch him." Just like they don't hear us, I wasn't trying to hear her. "The hell we can't." I wanted to know who-done-it. Where were they? I was going to kill 'em. Brynn wiped her eyes with her shaking hands, but the tears were relentless.

"What happened?" Her voice cracked as she attempted to yell.

The woman covered his body.

"I'm Detective Fayola Ojo. Let me help you up," she held out her hand. Brynn held the back of Cory's head.

"Answer me, what happened, and why are his pants down like that?"

"Come with me," the detective gestured toward an ambulance, "we weren't sure if you were alive at first."

Brynn closed her eyes and took a deep breath. Her tears fell onto what was left of his forehead. There was nothing she could do. She grabbed his hand, bent over, and kissed his fingers. She finally acknowledged the detective, replying to her last statement, "You wished I were dead."

The detective fumbled her words, "No, we... You looked... We assumed..."

Brynn interrupted, "It wasn't a question. Who would shoot him in the face like that and then leave him lying there like a dog?"

Instinctively, Detective Ojo glanced at a nearby squad car. "I'm not at liberty to say, but don't worry, we'll figure it out."

Brynn saw the glance out the side of her eye. "No need to pretend. You already know."

I wanted them to burn. I wanted them to roast. A hog roast. At the ambulance, the detective looked at Brynn.

"How did you sleep through that anyway?"

Brynn sat at the edge of the ambulance. She stared at the detective as she wiped her eyes with her middle finger. I loved it when she threw subconscious insults. The detective kept probing.

"I've never met someone that can sleep through multiple gunshots at such proximity without being under the influence."

We were under the influence, all right. Drunk from power.

"Do you want to drug test me? Make me walk the line and say my ABCs. I'm not drunk. Wouldn't you know if I were? Isn't that your job?"

Detective Ojo continued to question her. "Where were you coming from tonight?"

"The park."

"Which park?"

"Wade Walker."

"You sure about that? I heard about some ruckus at Southern Peaks not too long ago and I noticed a bit of blood on the back of your shirt."

Brynn changed the subject. "I just remembered something. Before I fell asleep, he said someone was following us with their headlights off. Maybe it was one of these cops. Why are there so many here? Something feels off. Why is he hiding in his car?"

"I understand what you're going through, but let's not play the blame game. What were you doing at the park?"

"It's a park. Why do I need a reason? Why am I being questioned when your killer is right there? And he better be in the backseat, headed to jail."

A nearby dumpy officer overheard the conversation and waddled over. "You might want to nix the accusations, little lady... Before I have to put you in a backseat. Is that what you want?"

Detective Ojo got louder, "Hey, let's not get ahead of ourselves. I'm asking the questions."

"I'm just saying, little lady's got a big mouth on her."

"Can you please remove yourself while I do my job? It's late, we all want to go home."

The officer walked off, lingering nearby. The detective whispered to Brynn. "Listen, I can help you, but I still need to do my job." She continued. "After he mentioned a car passing, what did he do?"

"I said it was following us, not passing, and I also said I was asleep after that, so I have no idea what he did or didn't do."

Was she actually trying to help us or was she trying to make up a story to help her kind?

"You aren't listening to anything I say." Brynn whispered, "incompetent."

Dumpy interjected again, grabbing Brynn's forearm, "What did you say? That's it. You're under arrest."

She snatched back. "You can't arrest me. I didn't do anything."

He was clearly out of pocket. The strands of my soul started twitching. I was thirsty and seeing red, but I knew it wasn't the right time. Not with all those cops close by.

"You have the right to remain silent and I'd prefer it. Anything you say can be used against you..."

Adlibbing the Miranda rights. Is that legal? As Brynn disengaged, dumpy's voice ebbed into the background and she was placed into the back of his car. *It's hot back here. I hate backseats. They're nauseating.* She watched out of the window as Cory's lifeless body was loaded into the ambulance. Brynn let her anger get in the way of her duty, and duty to the people comes first. Who could blame her? Waking up to death is her worst nightmare. Even though she couldn't have saved him if she wanted to, that doesn't stop her from beating herself up. *If I wasn't sleeping, I could have saved him. I could have stopped them. I hope they didn't...* She couldn't even bring herself to think the word. Her stomach knotted up. She'd hoped they hadn't ... Raped him. Nasty fuckers. *I wonder how many of them were there? Did they gang up on him? Did the others watch? Filthy pigs.*

Dumpy plopped behind the wheel. "Why are you people always starting stuff?"

"You people?" Insulted, Brynn snapped out of her thoughts.

"Don't you have anything better to do with your time than always getting into trouble?"

"Don't you have anything better to do with your time than harassing us people?"

"Watch your mouth, or you'll end up like your friend."

I could've killed him right then, right in that moment. Nobody would've ever known. How would they? They didn't even ID Brynn.

"So, it was you. You killed Cory?"

He took a sharp left turn unexpectedly, and she slid to the other side of the car, busting her bottom lip on the door. "Asshole, you didn't buckle me up."

"Oh, I didn't?" he said sarcastically. "You've got thick skin. You can take a little bruising."

What is that on the floor? I hope that ain't what I think it is. Is that a tooth on the floor? Is that real? Where's the body? Where's he taking me? I should kill him. Right here. Right now. She used her head as leverage to help herself up. Sucking the blood from her lip, her eyes beamed into the back of his head.

"I'll tell you what. I'll buckle you up at the next stop light. In the meantime, let me play some music for ya. How about one of my favorites, Bind Torture Kill by Suffocation?"

"A little intention with your obvious?" He was an idiot. I wished I could tell him, but I had something better. I reached through the cage, clasping his neck, squeezing it tight like the belt around his waist. The car jolted and he grasped at the door handle to escape. His clammy sausage skin was so easy to clutch. It felt like I was compelled, like holding one of those squishy sensory toys. I couldn't stop. I squeezed tighter, wrapping more hair around his neck like rings, wringing his neck. I hoped his head was going to pop off.

"I'll show you bind, torture, kill by suffocation," I said, but only my intentions were heard. He gasped for air, grabbing at his vest for something, anything, a pocket knife. He stabbed at me, all the while losing consciousness. Imagine someone stabbing at some hair wrapped around their neck. "Be careful, you might kill yourself." I chuckle now, thinking about it. His eyes bulged and he tried to take a breath. "That's my oxygen." I said. His hand dropped and at the last moment, Brynn felt sorry for this sap. She let go. He regained awareness, and the realization hit that he'd gotten more than he bargained for. He caught his breath, "What was that? I wasn't really going to kill you. I was talking out of my ass."

"Well talk out your mouth next time." I didn't play about Brynn's life.

He rubbed his neck. "Besides, I thought it was just hearsay."

"It?" Brynn asked.

"Root-witches. I thought they were just rumors to scare white folk. What am I saying? What did you do to me, girl?"

What I did to him was the same thing I did to that creep that grabbed Brynn. I altered his mood, taking the evil out of his heart. It was temporary and it differed slightly with each person. For Dumpy, it also made him tell the truth.

Basically, it made him calm the fuck down and keep it real.

"Girl? Even in fear, the bigotry still shines through, huh? Pathetic. Take me to jail."

At the jail, he pushed Brynn through the doors. Another officer awaited. He towered over Brynn. I noticed a Celtic cross tattooed on his inner right arm. The dumpy officer left a tip with him, "You better watch this one. She's feisty. Might need solitary." He nodded as if more was said in those few words than what was heard.

10
BONDING

May 28, 2020

Georgia was surprisingly tall, rarely smiled, and never seemed to worry or get flustered. She wasn't a woman of many words. Without having to do much, her presence was commanding. She had been growing her hair for years but I had never known her to cut it. Get a few trims, sure, but that's it. Her hair was frostbitten from seventy winters, apart from a patch of black on the side. It was interesting, considering most folks had patches of salt-and-pepper until they went fully grey. She usually kept it in a bun atop her head. Think messy bun, but somehow neat and contained. She's been wearing it like that forever. Grandma Georgia, or GG, as Brynn called her, raised her children with a hands-off approach. That's how she raised Brynn after the incident. Brynn used to love climbing trees when she was younger. She knew they protected her, their eyes were always blinking between the crevices in the bark, watching her. One day, GG must've known Brynn was going to fall because she stood there watching as Brynn climbed. One hand on her hip and the other up to her mouth, puffing a Newport. She didn't tell her to get down. Instead, when Brynn fell, she asked, "How was the landing?" She didn't wait for an answer. She turned around, went back inside, and continued watching The Young and the Restless, or maybe The Bold and the Beautiful. I can't remember, but it was one of those white people's shows. That's what GG called shows with a majority white cast, even though that's all she watched.

Outside of the jail, GG handed Brynn her keys. Brynn didn't reach out to take them.

"I don't feel like driving."

GG was unyielding, "Drive. I don't like to drive in the dark."

"The sun is almost up, though. And how did you get here so fast?" Asked Brynn.

"Don't worry about it. I worked my magic." GG always said that when she didn't want to answer something. The road glowed from the street lights and fog, and small pieces of rock and dirt were carrying themselves to somewhere beyond the grass, getting out of the way of the morning traffic. Brynn cranked the car, then looked at GG, "How did you know I was here?" GG pointed at the road, "Girl, drive. You got a lot of questions for someone that should be answering 'em. I think you owe me an explanation for why I had to get out the bed to bail you out of jail."

Brynn pulled off and turned right on Memorial Dr. "How much do I owe you for bail?"

Thank goodness it's Thursday because she probably would have left us here longer if it were a Sunday. GG went to church religiously, pun intended. She even went to Wednesday night Bible Study, but part of me believes she partakes to get out of the house. Being the eldest of twelve and a widow, I'd imagine she misses the companionship.

"I asked how you got arrested?" GG asked matter-of-factly, and Brynn responded without thinking, "huh?"

GG smacked her teeth, "huh, hell. You heard me." Brynn got ruffled, "GG, I was in the back of his squad car, and he said he was going to kill me. Was I supposed to let him?"

GG clasped her hands, "You were already under arrest then. That's still not an answer. Did he attack you?"

Brynn hesitated, "no, but -"

"Then you look like the violent one, the aggressor."

"There was someone's tooth on the floor of his car, Grandma."

"Be glad it wasn't a tongue. What happened at the park?" Yo! Grandma was wildin.'

Brynn looked at GG with scrunched brows. "How do you know about that?"

"I have my ways."

"This white lady said I bit her. Well, she said my hair bit her, which makes no sense. Then before I know it, white people were chasing us out of the park." And I would've done it again.

"What did you do, Brynn?"

"He's fine."

"That's not what I asked."

"I didn't do anything. I just made a path out of the park. Between Jacqori, the park, and the tooth, I figured I was next." Brynn thought back to the car incident, and her voice cracked, "I think he killed Jacqori, and no one seems to care but me." She started sobbing, and the car was totaled with silence. Grandma Georgia was never good at showing affection. She knows what to say, but the words get swallowed back down. She only imagines herself hugging her granddaughter because that's probably what they both need. Yet, the action is never actualized. Minutes feel like hours. The silence is loud. Meanwhile, I'm just sitting there, uncombed and untidy.

We finally got home. Before Brynn could open the car door, GG handed her a small white box with a pink satin bow.

"I have something for you."

"What is it?" She sniffled, wiping the tears with her inner thumb.

"You can open it when you get inside. One more thing, you can't trust folks. Everybody ain't your friend. Cut the cape."

"GG, I'm twenty-one. I think I know that by now." Brynn stuffed the box in her backpack purse.

"Pfft. You're still wet behind the ears. There are things you don't know... Or understand. People will smile in your face and stab you in the back." She shook her head as if she knew something.

"I prefer they frown in my face while stabbing me in the front," Brynn tried to make a joke, but GG didn't laugh.

"Sometimes, a decision must be made. It's you or them, them or us, life or death."

Brynn stopped what she was doing and propped her hands up on her purse, "You're starting to worry me, Grandma."

"Don't worry, keep your friends close and your enemies closer." GG got out of the car. "That's all you can do."

Brynn hugged GG as they met at the front of the car. "Is that why your best friend is white?" Brynn smirked and tried to laugh it off.

"You think you too grown to get smacked? You're not. Make sure you bring my chow-chow next time you come over. I want it for the BBQ."

Brynn waved, "Okay, love you, GG. Drive safe."

Georgia smiled, "Oh, I'm GG again."

Brynn dragged herself upstairs to her 3rd-floor apartment, each step more laborious than the last. Marc had been texting since she was at the park, and she hadn't responded for many good reasons, but he didn't know that yet. I'm sure he didn't have the same ways of figuring things out that GG had. I wondered what she meant by that.

11
SPLIT ENDS

May 28, 2020

Brynn moved into her one-bedroom apartment three years ago, it was to get out from under GG's thumb. She wanted to make her own rules in her own space. Her apartment was her shell, her sanctuary, her silence from the world. She'd livened it up with rainbow-hued decor, pop art prints, and a color-blocked abstract rug. The bedroom had a pink and yellow scheme. The vibe was happy. That was her goal in life then, happiness. But so much for that. Marc had about a trash bag's worth of clothes that he rotated through, and that trash bag had been sitting in the corner of Byrnn's living room for the past year. Marc wasn't the most attractive guy Brynn had ever met, he had a mustache and some under-chin hairs that would never quite grow into a full beard, and sometimes he had a funny smell, or at least that's what I thought. When he worked, it was part-time, and the job seemed to change every few months. Everything he did, he did with laze. They met about two years ago, through a mutual friend that neither of them even hung out with anymore. In the beginning, it was fun vibes and new adventures. They were both goofy, laughing at everything. They listened to the same music, watched the same movies, and played the same video games, in the beginning anyway, until Brynn realized Marc didn't actually like video games. But anywhere she went, he followed behind. Without much being said, they fell into what was supposed to be a serious relationship. He was at her crib almost every day. So much so, that she gave him a key.

That morning, when she made it up the stairs and got inside, Marc was on the sectional with one foot up like he owned the place. The nerve. He greeted Brynn with a snappy tone, "Did you get my texts?" Brynn had just got out of jail and I could feel her tiredness, her grief. Her eyelids were heavy. Her heart felt tight. This wasn't what she needed right now. She took two steps and was about to close the door behind her, but then she paused, deciding between having this argument and telling him to get the fuck out. The door shut and she sat across from him on the couch.

"Yes, I got your texts while I was fighting for my life, and then I got arrested. My phone died while I was sitting in jail next to a crazy woman shouting 'YAH Bitch YAH' all night. Folks gotta chill, but that being said, I didn't get any sleep. So, that's what I'd like to do right now."

Marc paused Sports Central. "Why didn't you call me when you got arrested?"

"I was barely in that long. They hadn't even given me a chance to call anybody before my grandma showed up to bail me out. Anyway, the last time I needed you, you never answered."

"Who were you with yesterday?" Marc asked with a suspicious tone.

Brynn fiddled with her keys. "I went to Southern Peaks with Cory for some fresh air—"

He cut her off, removing his leg from the couch to sit up. "See. I knew you were with that bitch nigga."

"You are so disrespectful. Cory is dead. He died last night." She looked down at her keys, choking back the tears, knowing it would cause more problems if she showed her feelings for him. Marc sucked his teeth, "How'd that happen? Did kill him with yo' crazy ass hair?"

I know he didn't call me crazy. I'll show him crazy.

She mean-mugged him. "Why would you even say something like that?"

"I'm dead-ass. I'm trying to figure out what him dying got to do with you being locked up?"

"I was with him when he died."

"Doing what?"

She huffed, "I told you, we were at Southern Peaks."

"Stop playing with me, bruh." He hopped up from the couch, pointing at her with his hand sideways. He stood leaning a tad bit to the right like he was leaning against a wall. He always stood like that, like he didn't want to stand.

"He didn't just die at Southern Peaks, breathing in air. What was y'all doing?"

"We were leaving the park, and he was driving. I fell asleep, but when I woke up, he was..." She didn't want to say the word again. "Gone." She couldn't hold back the tears anymore. "He was lying there, not moving. They murdered him. The police murdered him."

Sometimes, when Brynn was upset, Marc would smile mirthlessly in the midst of the conversation. It was this lopsided smile with a raised brow and a lifted cheek, combined with a brief laugh even though nothing was funny. It was like he wanted to taunt her, to show her how little he cared. Maybe it was to piss her off and get her riled up because he was pissed off and wanted her to make a fool of herself.

"You crying over this nigga now?" He diverted his attention to the paused TV, smirking with that lopsided smile.

"Why you acting brand new? He was my best friend before we even got together. You know we've been friends since middle school."

"Your best friend, huh?" He snarked.

"The truth is, if you would go places with me, and answer the phone when I need you, then I wouldn't have had to go with him. But things are different now. And honestly, you're worried about the wrong thing. You should care about why the police killed another unarmed Black man. One after the other, back-to-back. They're not even scared. They're killing us, and only God knows who's next."

He stared at the paused screen again. Probably because he knew she was speaking the truth. He probably imagined himself lying on the ground had he come to the park instead. Brynn wiped her eyes,

"I heard about a protest happening Friday at The Capitol. I'm going. You should come."

"Remember, that's your friend." He pointed at her. "I don't know that nigga."

She shrugged. "You don't know any of them. What difference does that make?"

"You don't see me protesting over them either, do you?"

"I wonder why that is?"

"Because it doesn't matter." He threw his hands in the air. "What the fuck is it going to change? Y'all out here looting and rioting, making y'all selves look like idiots."

She rolled her eyes, tears flowing no more. "The pot calling the kettle black. Robbing, stealing. Ain't that what your cousin does? Don't you sell the stuff that he steals?" She clapped between each word, "What's. The. Difference?"

"You're funny, Brynn, you know that?" He said coldly.

"Yeh, and you're selfish."

"I tell you what. You do you, and I'll do me," he said.

Her eyes closed. The room felt stretched as the distance between them grew. His words sounded mumbled like she was underwater. She couldn't hear him. She didn't want to hear him, she wanted to go to her room, shower, cry into her pillow with the covers over her head, and fall asleep. She wanted to let the mattress do its thing, pulsing beneath her, as she sank into the springs all the way down, like quicksand. That way, when she woke up, she could live in denial, even if for a second, as she wished, hoped, and prayed that today was a dream. She opened her eyes as he continued.

"It is what it is. I'm not about to risk my life, and neither should you. You still ain't told me how you got arrested, but I'm sure it wasn't because you were fighting back. You'd rather protest."

That was the most he'd ever said. Most of the time, he can't even gather his words to say anything intelligible. Brynn wondered what he meant, *I fought. I fight. That's why I got arrested. He thinks that because I don't fight him, I'm weak. Maybe I didn't fight before, but I'm fighting now. He wasn't there. Why does it always have to be a fight anyway? Why is that the only option? Why does everything turn into an argument? What is he not getting? How could you not want to stand up for your own people? If we don't, then we're saying it's okay. It's okay to murder us, and we're saying we deserve it. No message is a message. Silence is a message. And that's not the message that I want to send. Fight back, he says. That's what the protest is for. Idiot.*

"What does that mean?" She asked.

Marc walked toward the door to leave. She turned toward him, trying to convince him one last time.

"I didn't expect someone like you, to be acting like this. That could have been your father. It could have been your brother. It could have been you."

"Why? Because you fucking them too?"

"You know what, Marc? I'm tired. I need to rest. Just leave."

So, he did.

Brynn snatched the remote from the couch and smushed her thumb into the power button. Her eyes closed again, still standing with the remote in her hand. The silence was decompressing. She could think for a moment. Breathe. The figures in the pop art prints hanging on the wall closed their curtains too, and quickly got into bed, while underneath the coffee table, the rug shimmied to sleep, breathing soundlessly along with Brynn, her chest rising and falling with each breath. She reminisced about the car ride with Cory. The sunshine drizzling through the window. His tenderness with her, the moment his hand lingered on top of hers, how warm his fingers felt then. His hand on hers. His hand *not* on hers. Nightfall. His body on the ground. His cold fingers. The pieces of him. The pieces. She grabbed her stomach, trying to soothe the woe weeping through her insides. *I can't do this.* Her eyes fluttered open to the black TV screen, it stared back at her, saying nothing. She took a deep breath, trying not to lose it.

12
STRAIGHTEN

May 28, 2020

Brynn went to sleep in her safe place. It was warm and comfortable, the mattress pulled her in, and the springs inside giggled gleefully. But the sensation of falling woke Brynn up from what ended up being a long nap. She flung herself forward into an upright position, the only sound that could be heard was that of her yelp. She prayed that Cory's death had been a dream. She had to get out of the silence. It was 4 PM. Brynn already had a hair appointment set and refused to miss it on account of the happenings. She had to do something, like she and Cory talked about in the car. She had to push herself. She wasn't going to write a book or be a politician, but she could go to the protest. It was tomorrow, and she needed to be ready. *I needed to be ready. We needed to be there.*

Brynn grabbed her purse, remembering the box. She was in no mood for things that served the purpose of making her happy, gifts. *I'll open this later.* She placed it in a kitchen junk drawer and left. The day was so drab and overcast that the trees lining the streets kept their eyes closed, refusing to wake up. The sun wasn't shining into the salon, energizing the mood like the last time we were here. The white-painted brick walls looked beige. There was still that smell of burnt hair, lemongrass, and ammonia. Snipped pieces of hair lay on the floor, writhing below Brynn's feet. *I heard of pouring one out for the dead homies, but leaving them here on the floor, that's just disrespectful... To me, anyway.*

"Sit back for me," Almara draped Brynn with the cape, her skin looked darker today.

"My bad." Brynn never leaned back in the chair. She always sat forward.

"Yeh, you be ready to take off on me." Almara chuckled, "It's all good."

Almara examined Brynn's hair, moving it slightly here and there as if it was contaminated. "You look like you've been through the wringer. What happened to your hair?"

Brynn thought back to the past 24 hours, *my hair, somehow, bit a white lady, I beat up a white man, Cory got shot, and I did nothing. I had to sleep on a dirty ass jail bench while a mentally ill woman yelled in my ear. That's what happened to my hair. I should be grieving, but Cory wouldn't want that.* Brynn didn't feel like going into that. Instead, she directed her attention to everything else. There was something new on the floor propped up against the wall, yet to be hung. A canvas pop art portrait like the one in Brynn's apartment caught her eye, it didn't match with the monochrome vibe. For a second, I thought I was tripping because it had all of the colors of the rainbow. I thought I was seeing shit again. Brynn pointed over to it,

"That's new, right? The colorful one. Who is that?"

"Trevor Noah. He's a comedian. Funny as hell. You ought'a watch him sometime."

"I might do that." Brynn focused her attention on a certificate hanging near the mirror. It read: "This is to certify that Almara Grique has completed the prescribed course of study in cosmetology."

"Where does your last name come from? It's unique."

Almara parted Brynn's hair. "What makes you ask that?"

"I was just looking at the certificate on your wall." Brynn pointed up.

"It's South African," Almara responded instinctively, sectioning Brynn's hair.

"I didn't know you were from Africa."

"Aren't we all?"

"Technically, I guess. Does it mean anything?"

There was a long pause before Almara responded. "Possibly."

"What does—"

Almara interrupted, "You're inquisitive today, aren't you?" Almara grabbed the grease, "what do you want?"

"I've been coming here since I was younger. We always talk about me. I figured we could talk about you today."

Almara snickered. Her mouth didn't fully open nor did the sides turn up all the way when she smiled. It was a shallow smile like it was fake, or maybe that was just her face.

"No, what hairstyle do you want?"

"Oh! I'm thinking of a high ponytail. The slick back genie look. I'm not in the mood to be doing much with it."

"Tops." She greased Brynn's scalp. "You got any plans for the weekend?"

"Tops?"

"Yeh, as in 'good, okay, cool, I got you.'"

"Oh, ok. This weekend? I heard there was a protest tomorrow. I'm going. That's why I need my hair in tip-top shape." Brynn had an ah-ha moment. "Oh, tip-top is the same as tops."

"Why do you want to protest?"

"For the same reason that you're perming my hair. Power for the people that I need to help."

"That's not—"

She stopped herself. I was curious to know what she was about to say. Was she not helping? That's the only thing that could've made sense. Brynn beat herself up. *Why did I bring up the protest? Now, I have to tell her about Cory.*

"What did you say?" Brynn asked.

"Nothing. You look like you were about to say something."

"Well, you remember that guy that brought me to my last appointment?"

"Yeh, the snack." She smacked her lips as if she could taste him.

"Yesterday he took me to the park, and when we were trying to leave, these white folks blocked the exit. I kinda... Uh... made them move with my hair. It took a lot out of me, so I passed out in the car. But when I woke up..." Brynn's eyes watered. "He was..."

Almara spent the chair to see Brynn's face. "He died? I think I heard about that on the news. I didn't realize."

Brynn sobbed quietly, trying to hold it in. "Yeh and the police claim they don't know who murdered him, but they do. They did it."

"What makes you think it was the police?"

Brynn got defensive and her tears withdrew.

"What makes you think it wasn't the police? They always killing us. Besides, I remember him saying a car was following us."

"Maybe somebody robbed him."

"Robbed him, and left his wallet and car? His Chevy Caprice? In Atlanta? I feel it in my bones. It was a cop."

Almara crinkled her nose, basing Brynn's scalp. "Also, you need to get rid of Marc. Why wasn't he taking you to the park?"

"That's a whole-nother story. He's been acting funny lately."

Almara shrugged. Brynn explained further.

"Long story short, I'm going to the protest because I need to fight."

"I wish we didn't have to fight and we could all just get along, be united as one," Almara said hopelessly.

"What message does that send?"

"It's not about a message, Brynn. You'll only be targeted at the protest." *What does she mean targeted? Is it because I'm black? Everyone there will be Black. She's Black. Does she mean because I have powers? How would anyone know about that unless I used them? If I ask, she'll be vague like she's been the whole time.*

"Well, if there's a target on my back then I'll be the sacrifice for the others."

"If the shoe was on the other foot, do you think they would do the same for you? Why don't you steer clear of trouble and keep using your powers for healing and helping? You know, for good. Use your hair for good."

"A protest is bad?" Brynn almost turned around but remembered she was getting her hair done.

Almara began to apply the perm. "Alexa, turn up the music," she told the virtual assistant.

"What's in it anyway?"

Almara smacked her teeth. "In what?"

"The perms? The relaxers?"

"You got more questions than a three-year-old."

"My doctor said perms cause hair loss and fibroids, which can prevent you from having kids. Said there's formaldehyde and ammonia in them."

There had to be something in that creamy-crack because I, for one, was feeling woozy. The music sounded screwed and chopped all of a sudden. It was difficult to see. I was in and out of consciousness. "I'm high again, y'all."

"Yeh. You said that the last time. In all my years, I've never heard of anything like that." Almara rubbed the relaxer on my new growth as she went on, "How could they be putting bad things in something that makes your hair look so beautiful?" She was right. I was beautiful.

"I don't know. I thought you might know."

"Like I said, it's been years since cosmetology school. I'd imagine there's a little of this, a lot of that, and maybe some magic." She sneered. "Nothing to cause infertility."

"Witch magic? Is that why they call us root-witches?"

Almara meticulously applied perm on Brynn's roots, straightening every strand, stopping only to respond between her pauses. "No, chile. Ain't none of that trickery black magic mumbo-jumbo. I mean the good kind, white magic."

I wondered, did she even hear herself?

"After the protest, I'm going natural. For now, I want to be able to protect my people if something goes down there."

"I figured that was coming." Almara rolled her eyes.

"You can still be my stylist, though," Brynn said enthusiastically.

"No, boo. That's not my calling." Who was she calling Boo? I didn't like her tone. Brynn looked around to see if anyone had heard their conversation. Rejection didn't look good on her.

"Go to that third bowl for me." Almara gestured toward the rinse station.

Brynn unlocked her phone while she waited on Almara.

Marc: So, you still going to your little protest?

Brynn: I already told you I was.

Marc: I'm just asking.

Brynn: Ok

We were at my favorite part—that shampoo massage. I felt like a queen and Almara was my lady-in-waiting. This was a rare moment when someone was taking care of us. She's getting paid to do it, but hell, if it ain't for money, it's for something because nothing's free in this world. Almara leaned over us at the bowl, rinsing the perm from me. Watching my strands twirl down the sinkhole made me sick. Brynn started asking questions again. She didn't want to be left to her thoughts.

"What's that perfume you're wearing?" That sounded weird. Almara probably thought she was trying to hit on her.

"Design," Almara answered, squirting shampoo in her hands.

"I thought so. My grandma used to wear it all the time." I would have kept that one to myself.

Almara raised her eyebrows, lathering me up. "If I didn't feel old before, I do now. Thanks."

"Oh, I didn't mean—"

"Alexa, shuffle songs by Ari Lennox."

As Brynn readied to leave, Almara reminded Brynn of the upcoming weather.

"Brynn, it's supposed to rain this weekend. Don't be out in the rain letting your hair get wet. You might have to skip the protest. Two days, 48 hours, then you're good." Why was she so adamant about Brynn not going to the protest? Anyhow, I thought that was a weird way to say goodbye.

13
FLYAWAYS

May 29, 2020

S it down. Shut up. Stop whining. Slavery is over. Racism doesn't exist. Let it go. You're stuck in the past. Get over it. He started running. She was acting hostile. He went for his pocket. She was acting suspiciously.

In the absence of listening, we march. We march to take a stand. We march for the past, and we march to the future. We march because of slavery because actions speak louder than words. We march to show up and show out. We silently contemplate the murders of our people. Shooting us in the back. Strangulation. Shooting us in the face, executing us one by one. Then smiling in our faces, telling us it's okay because we kill each other. We contemplate our lives changed. Mothers that won't sleep the same. Fathers that feel like they've failed. The blood doesn't just wipe off the walls. We empathize. We pray for a change. A change to laws that currently support the discrimination of people based on surface-level things. Qualities that do not predicate unfortunate connotations. Characteristics that highlight their guilt, shortcomings, and villainy. The shame is so deep-rooted and internalized that they take it out on us. Their actions are a mirror of contempt. They remain hyper-vigilant, protecting their power. We pray for their healing. We reflect on our actions. It's not our move, but still, we wonder what we can do to force a change. Should we have our license and registration already out? Should we walk, not run, in fear? The past has shown that to be hit or miss.

We hope. We meditate for healing in the presence of hate. We meditate to relax and stay calm. We meditate for balance and emotional well-being. To cope with stress and to refocus our attention on health. We meditate for equality and equity.

We arrived at Centennial Olympic Park when the sun was at its highest point and the asphalt streets still gulping down the heat. There was a moment of silence. The sun marinated on the melanin of every clenched, raised fist in the crowd. Brynn didn't bring a sign like the others. She wore a taffy pink shirt. On it was a black fist with a gold crown sitting atop. The words across the bottom read: *armed with a crown.* She felt like she was making a change and doing her part by being there. She wished Marc wasn't being so stubborn. *He should be here, taking part in the movement. Another voice would help. Seems like he was worrying for nothing because nothing is happening. Besides the feeling that we're talking to ourselves, this feels right.* People were everywhere. Mostly young, 20s and 30s. Some with long-sleeved shirts, some with no shirts, some with shorts, and some in jackets. Some seemed to be confused about the season. Even with Atlanta's erratic weather, that was weird because it was hot as hell, the heat was rippling through Brynn's sneakers all the way to her skin. I was sweaty, and I get bent out of shape when I'm hot. People walked around aimlessly like zombies. Folks were angry. Some smiled. Some laughed, and some stood there staring blankly. They were talking on their phones, sitting around watching others spray paint buildings. Leaning on trees, standing on cars. It was like TV static, white noise and black speckles.

A young white guy holding a mini news camera was interrupted by two random middle fingers blocking his shot. They wanted their fifteen seconds of fame. All the cameraman could do was laugh. Elsewhere, a man held up a sign that read: "When I was 11, I turned 13, because FUCK 12." Another with a sign that read: "Silence is betrayal." It was an amalgamation of characters and moods, but an alignment of duty. For the most part.

A woman walked by with a shirt that read *Black Lives Matter*, flaunting a fluffy twist-out, an expression of pride, her hair spoke volumes. There was a lovely wealth of hair everywhere—textures, lengths, colors, and styles of all kinds. Brynn passed by a woman with natural hair. *I wonder how she got it like that?* It reminded me of an afro, but super crinkly. I tried to make conversation with the passerby because I'd never spoken to other hair. I'd never tried before, I didn't even know if I could. I said, "Hey, girl, hey! I like your style. That must've taken quite a while, with yo' thick and *natural* curves." I got no response. I felt stupid. I don't know what I was thinking. If Brynn couldn't hear me, then neither could they. I wondered if that person's hair was like me. Then, I got nervous. *Maybe her hair can't speak.* Brynn kept talking about going natural! Would I be mute if she did? Was I going to disappear without the perm? What would happen to me? With all those questions, I started to sound like Brynn. I needed to chill.

Two boys were selling water out of a cooler. It was good to see them out here hustling, learning young, they seemed like irreplaceable skills for the future.

"How much for the water?" Asked Brynn.

"Two dollars," the younger one replied.

"I'll take two," she handed them a five.

The younger one gave her two bottles as the older one fumbled through his fanny pack.

"Keep the change. Thanks."

A nearby woman noticed. "They've been stiffing us all day."

"Stiffing you?" Brynn knew what she meant. She wanted the woman to make a fool of herself so that when she got smart, she was validated.

"Overcharging us."

"Two dollars for water and a little support sounds cheap to me, but okay."

The woman rolled her eyes. *Maybe she should've brought her own water.*

"Brynn, watch out!"

Brynn swiftly turned around as if something was coming for her. Her eyes squinted. *Am I losing it? I swear I just heard somebody say my name.* She noticed something out of the corner of her eye. She followed it, watching as it whirled through the air, over her head. It felt like slo-mo. It was like time stopped and everybody was supposed to see it. An apple. *Did somebody just throw an ambrosia apple at the police?* She was surprised. She knew it was an ambrosia because they were her favorite and they were pretty big. The cops try to dodge it, but they bump shoulders instead. The apple thunked one of them in the leg. That was going to leave a bruise. Brynn turned around to see who did it. I saw who it was, but I was unable to tell her. It was a guy with a skateboard. So much for a peaceful protest. It got silent for a split second, but then the crowd got riled up, "fuck the police, fuck the police." The cops form a line behind their shields. *This isn't good.* They respond, shouting over the megaphone:

"Leave at once. Battery against a police officer will cost you jail time."

Nobody moved. Someone found it amusing to yell, "All white people to the front." I lost it.

Brynn locked arms with two people beside her and nodded at the others to do the same. She led the crowd toward the police in solidarity. To change the tone, she shouted, "No justice, no peace." The people behind her repeated, "No justice, no peace," as they marched closer to the police. Reaching the blue barricade, they stood, staring, chanting. Now, it felt like we were talking to someone. It felt like we were getting our point across, but now Brynn was scared. *What if they devise some bogus police law that says we can't stand within six feet of the police? Approaching While Black or some shit. What if snipers start taking us out one by one?* She let the fear get the best of her.

BOOM!

That was something big, and it felt like it blew up. It became a distraction. The tense faces behind shields relaxed as we all looked away, but only for a moment since they, too, were unaware of the noise's source. We made our way toward the sound, where Brynn noticed a car engulfed in flames. The side read

'Atlanta Police Department.' *Wow, they weren't kidding about no peace.* Brynn's phone vibrated. It was the doctor's office. She watched the phone as it rang, stuffing it back in her pocket. *I'll call them back tomorrow.*

14
CROSSHAIRS

Almara - May 31, 2020

I didn't realize I'd been shot, something just felt off. There wasn't any pain at first. Just blood. I woke up the next morning in the same position I had been in when I fell asleep; on my back, shirtless, staring at the ceiling fan. Blood soaked my beautiful indigo and gold jacquard damask satin textured comforter, it was ruined. The pillows, shams, and window treatments matched it. Where was I going to find such a royal pattern again? I still had on my jean shorts and sneakers, and that darn yin-yang choker. I'd had the choker for so long that the white had become cream, the contrast more beautiful. It was made of faux pearls. I pulled it off my neck, it felt like it was suffocating me. Moving, even an inch, hurt like hell. But I had to. I stood at the mirror that hung over my dresser and waited for it to unfurl and show me my reflection. It did so reluctantly, and I twisted my body around to see the wound. The bullet was more visible than last night when I had last checked it. I was starting to heal, pushing the lead out. The skin around it was shifting. There was a quick knock at the door before it flung open.

"Erik! Damnit, you scared me."

He was wearing his full navy blue police uniform, donning a gun, pepper spray and baton. I found Erik to be a very confident guy. Some found him supercilious, but he meant well overall.

"You left me," I yelled bitterly.

"Who the fuck are you?" Taking a Weaver stance, he aimed his gun at me.

Usually, I would guise myself as white, but I was still in my base form. At this moment, it wasn't a preference, it was the result of being shot. When my body is focusing on healing, it won't let me do much else. It won't let me turn. In fact, if I am shifted while I'm hurt, my body always shifts back to base. Erik didn't know me as biracial. My curly red hair, the freckles on my cheeks and under my eyes, my light brown skin. He didn't identify with that, as he stood there with the gun pointed at me, I felt compelled to shift. I tried, even if only for a second, to force my face into an elongated oval shape with a skinny nose, and green eyes. My skin turned pale ivory. That's what he was used to seeing. I was unable to retain that look, but he recognized white-me. He knew that beyond this fair skin, was fairer skin.

"No need to shoot, I'm already shot. It's me," I said in a voice he recognized, enunciating every syllable.

His entire face crumpled and his ears stood up. He rushed over to me,

"What happened?" As he was about to touch me, he snatched back, "why is your skin moving like that?" The gun was still in his other hand, pointed at the carpet. He took a step back, "are you... One of them? A root-witch?"

"What is a root-witch? Where did you get that from?"

"I'm out in the field, we see things. More things than most. We talk."

"Sure." I was unconvinced. "And I'm healing, that's what my skin is doing. You know that thing everyone does. I just do it quicker is all."

"So, you can change the way you look and heal yourself. All this time, you never told me. What else can you do?"

"That's about it. That's why I never told you," I glanced at the gun. "You planning on shooting me or putting that thing away?"

He put the gun on the dresser and crossed his arms, "I came back for you, but I couldn't find you."

"Huh?"

"The protest. After I went to check on that officer, I came back and you were gone." He quickly uncrossed his arms. "I heard one of them was at the protest stirring up shit."

"One of them? The police?"

"A root-witch. They're so violent. You're not like that, are you?"

I was half-offended. I didn't know whether to take up for them or agree.

"Yeh, I get it. A Black woman killed my parents," I blurted without thinking. Then, I tried to clean it up, "But they're not all bad."

"How?"

"My mother was Black. She wasn't bad."

"No, I mean, how did this woman kill your parents?"

"She murdered them."

"I guess it couldn't have been that bad, since you don't want to tell me."

First, he was going to shoot me. Now, he was gaslighting me. I walked to the bathroom, wet a hand towel, and handed it to him to help wipe the dried blood.

"You're so confused," I said.

He dabbed it. "I'm just trying to understand."

I turned around and snatched the towel, standing in front of him, unable to decide which of his eyes to focus on, the green one or the grey one. When people say you should look someone in the eye, I don't get how. It would be my attention hopping from one eye to the next. He was such a distraction. Such a handsome idiot. He sensed my desire and my irritation, then changed the subject only for a moment.

"Mara, you know you don't need to be white or change for me?" I rolled my eyes because that was a crock of shit.

"Don't I, though?"

"I know the real you."

"Do you, though?"

"We've been together long enough," he kept trying to convince me.

"What's long enough?" For me, he was a momentary boy toy. I liked him, but I've had too many years on this Earth to be fully committed. He couldn't last my lifetime.

"Stop it. I know you. You can wear the skin you were born in."

I snubbed him with my good shoulder and walked to the other side of the room. Grabbing an old t-shirt out of the drawer, I felt the need to cover up.

"When I look like this, of course, you know me. Every skin you see me in is me. Who I look like or the shape I take doesn't matter. For all you know, that light brown skin and curly hair could have been another person I shifted into."

"That's some fine imagination you got there," said Erik.

"Fine, huh? Don't tell me you've been secretly fantasizing about Black women."

"Stop it, you know that's not what I meant." His face turned red.

"A mixed woman is probably the closest thing you'll ever get to screwing a Black woman without feeling shame, but still white enough that you feel safe. I'm cat nip, a fly-by-high."

"Are you drunk, woman? Tell me how your parents died."

He didn't want to let this go. I wondered why. "Suddenly you need understanding? To lessen your guilt? Or are you just adding it to your list of reasons to get rid of them?"

Erik tilted his head sideways and stared at me.

"Fine." I sat on the edge of the bed, near the nightstand. "You really want to know?"

"Shoot."

"I'll leave that up to you."

Erik sat in the indigo wing chair I had in the corner of the room, pretending I didn't just make that comment.

"Okay, well, you know about 400 years ago, when the Dutch colonized South Africa?"

He nodded.

"Well, that colonization led to mixed-raced people, and they were referred to as the Griquas. About 200 years later, a full San man named Andries Waterboer was elected Kaptein of Griqualand West. He was calm, inescapable, cruel, and worst of all, patient."

"San?"

"Black. Most Kapteins were biracial, but Waterboer was literate and calculating, so he found a way around that."

"I thought all Blacks were slaves."

"You probably also think Columbus discovered America."

"1492," he agreed. I swooped my hand over my head to insinuate where the point went.

"Like I was saying. He was ruthless, and his principles caused a split between the Griquas. Some stayed west and some went east. There was a group of nomadic Griquas that called themselves Basters."

"Bastards?"

"Did you hear a 'D' because I didn't use the letter 'D.'"

"Calm down. I can see the wrinkles on your face," he sneered.

"Whatever," I scoffed. "Baster, with an R, means mixed breed in Dutch."

"Ok, go on."

"Well, Waterboer had a very powerful mistress. Like, actual powers. Like me."

"It's just one trick. How can one shapeshifter be more powerful than another shapeshifter?"

I sighed. "I didn't mean exactly like me. Only mixed women can shift. His mistress was also full-San, and they're born with various abilities that originate from their hair, like the girl from the news."

"Whoa, whoa, whoa." He leaned up in the chair. "All Black women have powers?"

"Just some."

He leaned back in his chair again. "Well, now. That's interesting... Go on."

"His mistress helped him defeat armies and win wars. What we would later learn is that she helped massacre every warrior that was sent to battle, including my parents. No more hugs, no more love, no home, she took everything from me."

"I'm sorry to hear that. What... What was your mother doing there?"

"She was one of the nurses."

"If your dad was white. Why was he with the Basters?"

"Because of me."

"Wait. Hold on, wait. Are you trying to tell me that you're 200 years old?"

"I thought you knew me?" I taunted him. "A true woman never reveals her age. Anyway, I answered your question. I hate talking about it. It's not natural for one person to possess that much power over others. I wish I could rewind time and stop her." I looked down for a second. I needed a moment. Though it had been forever, it still bothered me that I was robbed of something everyone else got to experience. It wasn't fair.

"If you give a nigger an inch, he will take an ell. That's what my grandfather always told me," Erik digressed.

I launched from the bed, annoyed. "I told you not to use that word around me." I wasn't stupid enough to think he would never use it, but I deserved some respect.

"You're saying the same thing." He threw his hands in the air defensively, like someone was pointing a gun at him, like he was the victim. Everything I said went in one ear and out of the other. I shook my head. "We should all be equal so that no one can destroy so many lives. We should all get along as my parents did. Be in love, not war. Maybe hundreds of years down the line, we can all be one. One race."

Erik clicked his tongue. "I don't want my grandchildren and their children's blood to be tainted with that savagery."

My teeth smacked. "There it is." He thought I was some bitter bitch, emotional for revenge. Maybe I was savage, but if I was, it was because it was in my blood. Part of it, anyway. "I need to wash up, so we can wrap this up anytime."

"Hey, I'm just saying. That girl from the news bit someone and slammed a man into a truck… With her hair."

"Again, all Black people aren't bad, just the ones with too much power. And I didn't hear anything about a bite. I thought the news said she threw him across the parking lot or something."

"Tom-ay-to. Tom-ah-to," he stood up.

I walked to him and delicately put my hand on his vest. "Hold on, do you know something that I don't know?" He looked up at the ceiling.

"I just need to find her, to see what she knows." He said.

"Is that why you went to the protest? So, you can find a girl… A Black girl? And what was your plan when you found her? Kill her in front of thousands of people? I thought you were getting paid as security to go to that protest. Like a part-time thing."

I stopped talking, noticing his ripped pocket. My eyes narrowed. The whole time I was talking, he didn't seem concerned about my past. He didn't seem surprised when I mentioned the girl from the news. He knew exactly what happened at that park, almost like he was there, and not too long after the park thing, a boy was killed in the same vicinity. That's what Brynn was telling me about. It was Cory.

"Oh, my God! It was you," I snatched my hand down. "That boy that was shot that night. And they said there was a girl in the car. You killed him! You are a fuckin m—"

He interrupted me, stepping closer with a low, stern voice. "Almara, now I tried to have a civilized conversation with that boy. He became unrestrained and out of control. My life was on the line."

He wanted me to believe it was self-defense. I couldn't believe it. Why act secretive if it was self-defense? He was the bitter savage, unbelievably savage. I could tell he was lying because of the rapid blinking. I felt my nose tingle. "So, I'm dating a murderer? A dirty cop?"

"I'm doing what I have to do to protect myself, Mara."

I stopped walking. "Don't call me that. I'm tired of the violence. This isn't the way to fix it."

He turned around, stepping in my face with a look of epiphany about what I'd been doing. "The hair," he said. "Manipulation is better?" He was insinuating something about me. About what I do as a hairstylist. I am what I am but I'll use what I got to make this world a better, fairer place to live.

"It's more passive than aggressive," I professed, "but violence doesn't fix it."

"It's a weak move," he poked my forehead, "and nobody likes a passive-aggressive bitch."

He'd never acted like this before. Never had he put his hands on me unlovingly. He'd never talked to me like this before.

"I take it your life wasn't on the line then?" I asked, already knowing the answer.

Erik put his hand in front of me to stop talking. I backed up, putting space between us, and pointed at the door. I was rethinking everything I thought he was, a protector, sympathizer; I thought he was here for me. I was wrong. He's selfish like everybody else. Maybe, he too, has too much power. Even as time passed, what he said echoed in my mind, and as the days went on, the pain left my body, and the ease of shifting returned. I stared at myself in the mirror now, I could feel it watching me, reflecting only parts of me when it felt like it. I liked to see myself change. I liked to see my fair skin transform into white and my golden-red hair, from root to tip, change to honey blonde. I liked to see my curls flatten, bone-straight. I liked to watch as my eyes went from brown to blue. After all these years, it was still a sight to see. Flipping my hair behind my shoulder, I walked out of the house, invigorated.

15
HIDE NOR HAIR

May 30, 2020

The flames ignited a fervor in some and unlocked a wildfire in others. But it made everyone go stupid.

"Give me back my hat," a cop yelled as he aimed his stun gun. "Get over here. You're under arrest." Short and doughy, he became the target of a prank.

"For what?"

"You're under arrest."

"For what?"

The cop fired. I heard a pop and a plop. The electroshock sent the man's tense body to the wet concrete and the little rocks on the floor shivered when his body hit the ground. A stun gun is considered a deadly weapon, yet here we are. Four cops rushed him. One was pushing his arm into the ground, another his legs, another had the cuffs, and the doughy cop had a knee in his back.

"Stop resisting. Where's my hat, asshole?" The man moaned in response, screaming from pain. "I can't hear you. Where's my fucking hat?"

Afraid to speak up, a man in a rainbow tie-dye shirt lifted his umbrella slightly and said, "he doesn't have your hat. Another guy took it and ran off. You tased the wrong person. You've got the wrong guy."

"Get back," flustered, feeling like an idiot, the cop darted to his squad car. The engine revved like he thought it was in gear. *I know he's not about to do what I think he's about to do. I know he is not.* The cop threw the car in gear. Before he stopped to think, he had already slammed his foot on the gas pedal, facing a group of people. The tires screeched and spun before the car took off, giving everyone a moment to realize what was happening. People dove for their lives, running towards the sidewalk, grabbing friends and loved ones. He appeared panicked, but the car was still going. Instinctively, Brynn ran toward the car, pushing through, screaming, frantic people, hoping to stop him. Apparently, we weren't hiding anymore. *I can't let him kill these people and then claim self-defense later. But damn it, it's raining. The rain gon' mess up my perm, and if I try to stop this car, I could pass out again. Who knows what he'd do to me in my vulnerable state? All that might be left of me is a tooth.*

I didn't like getting wet. Dancing at the club, swimming in a pool, having sweaty sex, sitting in a sauna, or standing in the rain... Those are things that Black women don't do. It's not that they don't want to do those things, their hair wouldn't appreciate the gesture, and neither would their hairstylist, especially after that hairstylist gave fair warning, which, Almara did. Doughy abruptly stopped of his own volition. Standing outside the driver-side window, Brynn gave him the look of a disappointed mother. I slinked into the car, pressing the brake to take control. His leg flinched away from me.

"So, you were trying to take everybody out? All at once, huh?" Brynn asked him.

He picked up his radio, "root-witch spotted on Centennial and Marietta. I repeat, root-witch spotted. Request backup."

"Why would you do that? You've got backup right there." She gestured at the other three cops, using me as a pointer. His focus shifted to me as he glared at me in repugnance. He unbuckled his gun holster and we ducked immediately. He shot out of the window without aim. I grabbed his wrist and the gun fell. Brynn tried to remain calm despite his best efforts to piss us off.

"Best you can do is get out of the car. This ain't what you want." I started to think, maybe this was what he wanted. Maybe he wanted these hands. We let go but he didn't get out of the car.

Brynn sighed, "ok, bet. I'll tell you what..." I knew what she wanted, so I touched his shoulder to relax him, and she went on, "...You sit tight, take a chill pill. Wait on back up." Brynn threw up air quotes. "Or whoever." He sighed in relief as we walked away. *This can't be life. Your job is to protect and serve, and you drive a two-ton vehicle into a crowd of people.*

"I thought for sure we'd be down for the count after all of that." *I swear, I'm hearing voices. That, or I can hear myself think louder than normal. No, it must be all these people. All the chatter.* A bystander pointed at me.

"Look! Did you see her hair? Oh shit, she's like an enchantress or some shit." Someone else shouted, "Worldstar!" And Brynn ran into a nearby parking deck before others started to pay attention. It was difficult to pick us out of the crowd, so long as I looked normal. So, shouting 'Worldstar' was useless. *Everybody's got a name for what I am. Everybody's got a judgment. Root-witch, enchantress, demon-hair, none of which I asked for. I'm just out here trying to save lives, but I'm the demon? I'm the witch?*

"They're ungrateful." I thought, they should be thanking us.

So ungrateful. How about saying Thank you? The resemblance in our words was uncanny. Could it be? After a few moments, Brynn peeked out and saw a woman bent over. I couldn't tell what was wrong with her at first. She seemed afraid to move. All I could see were jean shorts and long, blonde curls dangling in front of her. She was holding her shoulder, yelling,

"What happened? Help me. I think I've been shot." She screamed, "Erik!"

Looking around for a male figure, I didn't see what I presume an 'Erik' to look like coming to help, or anyone for that matter. Brynn being Brynn, she couldn't bear to see anyone in pain, even blondie. We rushed over and guided the woman by the elbow. "Walk with me. What's your name?"

"Al..." The woman trailed off. She thought about it for a moment as if she didn't know her own name. I guess I might forget my name too if I'd been shot. She finally answered, "Alice." I snagged a bite of blood before we tried to heal her, I was parched in this heat. The flavor wasn't as privileged as what I expected for a white woman. It was sweet, then sour. Something was off. I lay against Alice's shoulder to heal her. She lifted her head, she had a face like a doll and a yin-and-yang choker around her neck. Her eyebrows scrunched. I didn't put it together then, but she recognized us. She wasn't shocked by our presence. Brynn pulled her closer.

"You can lean on me. I saw some police right around this corner. They'll take care of you." Brynn guided her to a less crowded area. I could hear Alice's heart beating faster when Brynn mentioned the police. Maybe it was the adrenaline from being shot. I continued healing her, I could tell that's what Brynn wanted. Alice crinkled her nose as she gabbled,

"I'm not going to make it before I... I need to sit down for a minute."

I wasn't having that. "No, ma'am. No, honey. You will not die on us. They will say we killed you, a white woman. No questions asked—just prison, straight like that. Not today, Satan."

Alice's knees gave. She almost fell, but we caught her and eased onto the ground for a rest. Again, our abilities didn't seem to surprise her. Brynn tried to grab her hand but she snatched it away, irritated. So Brynn sat with her instead, making her lay her head against Brynn's shoulder. Suddenly blondie wasn't so blonde anymore. The night was approaching, so I couldn't be sure, but her hair appeared more of a golden red. The wrinkles under her eyes revealed age, it was as if her complexion had changed too, but again it was dark outside. Brynn looked at her and did a double-take.

"Your hair," she whispered, "are you one of... Are you a... Never mind." She wondered if Alice had powers but didn't know how to ask, and didn't want to offend her, the way we'd been offended so much. Brynn ran her fingers through Alice's hair, wishing she could have held Cory in these moments before he died. She wished she could have told him she loved him and kissed him on the forehead. Brynn was startled out of her regrets by Alice's cries,

"Oh my God, Oh my God." It was awkward, to say the least.

Brynn insisted they keep moving together, motioning to the other side of the street. "Just make it to that sidewalk, and I'll go get them."

"Okay," Alice stumbled across, barely standing straight, then plopped back down once there. "Okay, go now. Go get them," she demanded. But when we returned, she was gone. It would seem that I was able to heal her more than I thought, or maybe she was faking it. The protest was still kicking off on the streets, and I could hear more sirens faintly approaching, wailing with threat. Heat was rising off of the earth like white flames. Brynn felt hot and watched. That's when she felt his presence, and turned to see Marc standing behind her.

"What are you doing here?" she asked with a lackluster tone.

He stood there, not talking, looking like a lost puppy, so she yelled at him, "Spit it out!"

16
BREAK BONDS

May 30, 2020

Marc walked closer to Brynn and I felt her temperature increase with each step. She could feel her anger boiling over, and she didn't know how he was going to take that. He was lurking around like a tiger, and the lack of people nearby made her uneasy. Finally, he opened his mouth,

"What are you doing here?"

Feeling fed up, she got belligerent. She threw her hands in the air and looked to the left, then looked to the right, as if the answer wasn't obvious. The protest, duh. Less tolerant, she asked again, "Why the fuck are you here?" It was like she was me, candid and sour.

"I wanted to make sure you were good."

She felt the need to be sarcastic, "You wanted to make sure I was good? You didn't care before, so why don't you keep that same energy? No, you didn't want to make sure I was good. You wanted to check up on me, like a stalker," she said scornfully.

Marc barely made eye contact, instead, he focused on the graffiti, the trash on the ground, the nearby bushes, anything but Brynn.

"Shawty look—" She couldn't help but interrupt because fuck his feelings.

"I'm looking, but I don't see anything."

He went on, "Let me finish. I wasn't trying to hear about that shit at the time. My girl, with some other nigga, ignoring me, and then she gets locked up. How did you expect me to act?"

"I expected you to at least hear what happened. You just went straight defensive and accusatory. Some racist shit went down at the park, and I couldn't just stop to text you back in the middle of it..." She paused with a revelation. "Oh, I get it now. That's why you're here. You saw the news."

"I thought you were fucking around on a nigga."

"You thought wrong, thinking ass nigga," that's what I would have told him, but that's just me, little ole Brair.

"You ain't loyal. You ain't faithful. You think I'm stupid?" Brynn said.

"What you mean?" He huffed, swaying his body slightly right.

"You text bitches. You text bitches when I'm in the same room as you. You think I don't know you're texting females when you think I'm not paying attention? Smiling at the phone and shit. Turning it face down. I'm always paying attention. And you know what, you don't answer every time I call. Hell, had you been around, you could have been with me at the park instead of Cory, but you were probably somewhere fucking some bitch."

"You trippin right now. Ain't no other bitches."

"Ask him about Jessica." I'd hoped Brynn would get my drift.

"So, ain't no Jessica?" she asked him.

"And Natasha."

"Ain't no Natasha?" She went on.

"And Rashida." I was full of names and it didn't bother me to remind her.

"Oh, and what about Rashida? Did I make those names up, huh? Did I pull 'em out my ass?" She hiked her butt slightly and made a one-hand motion like she was pulling something out of her butt. She didn't need him, but she wasn't trying to hear that. He was a detriment to her mental.

"Marc, I need space," she said. He took a step back, assuming she meant physically. "No. I mean, I need space from you for a while—space from this relationship because this ain't it."

He opened his hand, reaching for her, and when she stepped back, his forehead wrinkled. "That's how it's gone be?" With people like him, it wasn't the betrayal that bothered them. It was the lack of control. He wasn't getting his way, and he was about to start pouting. Marc started up, "so, you just going to leave me hanging after everything we've been through? You always quit."

"I always quit? Walking out while we're trying to talk ain't quitting? Shutting down and giving me the silent treatment ain't quitting? Talking to bitches behind my back ain't quitting? You'll talk to them more than you talk to me. You've been quiet, and that's quitting. I'm just doing what you refuse to do."

He smiled mockingly. "Why are you being so emotional?" He tilted his head to the side and slightly backward, like he did when he was bothered, but couldn't come up with the words to make his point. He didn't want to make a scene in front of people. "Ain't no such thing as space. We're either together or we're not," he declared. Mister Ulterior-Motives had ultimatums. Imagine that.

"We're not," she said unemotionally.

"You know you trippin' right?" Marc paced back and forth.

"You know you said that already? Anyway, what difference does it make? You got hoes. You don't need me."

"Okay, Brynn," he put his hands together in front of himself and then quickly separated them. He walked toward her and grabbed her shoulder, aggressively pulling her toward him. The veins in his neck protruded. "You know what? Fuck it. Fuck you," he grumbled through his teeth. He pushed her and she had to catch her balance. I thought if I gave him a little shove back, he'd know what was up. Brynn thought, *maybe I should de-escalate. Nah! I want to know how he really feels. I want to see the asshole come out. I'm tired of trying to change his mood. Help him be a better person. Fix him. I'm tired of being the bigger person. He needs to be responsible for his actions and his words. People around here need my help, life or death help. This is petty shit, not worthy of my time.*

"Bye, Marc." She walked off with her back facing him to show what little she cared about him. To show she wasn't scared of him, but she was. Even with me having her back, she was scared. She was scared of missing out on things that I couldn't possibly provide. "Fuck him," I was mad. As we headed north toward the CNN center, a woman was in Brynn's direct path walking toward her. Brynn wasn't in the mood and neither was I. "We should trip her," I said.

The woman had on Crocs with a white shirt and some grey leggings. Her mom-hat only slightly contained her messy brunette hair. I hate 'em. I hate their pale skin and their rat voices, and the passive façade they put on. Their lanky bodies and droopy faces. I hate that they were born with advantage, joy, and privilege. I hate that they don't have to worry about leaving their houses without their ID. They don't have to worry about getting shot at a traffic stop. I hate their happy-go-lucky faces, prancing around living naïve, with no care in the world. I hate that they're a so-called delight to be around. They should all be flayed alive—the lot of 'em, but that's my opinion. I'm just hair. Brynn knew how rude folks could get, and even though she was hotheaded and ready to start some shit, she slid two steps left because she had had enough bullshit for one day. The brunette took two steps to the right. They were on the same path again. As she got closer, I noticed her smiling.

Brynn asked, "do I know you?"

The brunette giggled and wrapped her arms around Brynn, giving her an unsolicited hug. The woman squeezed lightly as if asking Brynn to return the favor. When she didn't, the brunette let go, and explained, "We're hugging Black women." Brynn was so focused on the woman being in her way that she didn't see the dozen other women around her heading toward other Black women, bombarding them with regard... Without regard. The brunette went on, "I just wanted to thank you for saving us."

I didn't save her.

17
CREW CUTS

Summer 1827

"Fools," he smirked at the loose smoke from their dinner campfires hovering in the treetops. He checked the pocket watch attached to his side. Then looked at his mistress standing behind him.

"It is time," he said.

While the warriors slept, Andries and his mistress, Nandipha, arrived atop a nearby hill, overlooking the Baster tents. Waterboer was a lanky, dark-skinned man with a full beard and a short, scruffy afro. He wore a top hat and had a long, flamboyant walking stick with knobs on each end. He always wore a patterned three-piece suit without a tie, no matter how hot it was, while his mistress, Nandipha, was a petite woman with hair the color of mulled wine. It was fluffy and tousled, so long that even shrinkage couldn't prevent it from resting on her shoulders. She stood behind him with her lip corner tightened, raised slightly, and her arms gently crossed with a mint green shawl draped across her body. The air was cool and smelt of burnt wood and evergreen. Only the scuttle of animals moving between the grass could be heard from where they stood.

"I said I wasn't going to help you unless you needed my help. What you are asking me to do is murder innocent people."

"My love. We agreed," Andries urged.

"I agreed to nothing," she calmly replied.

He thrust his body around, taking two large strides toward her. He stopped an inch from her face, slowly caressing his fingers up through the back of her head, against her scalp, and into the roots of her hair.

"Do this for me." He pleaded, looking down at her. "Have this egbreekster remove his hands from me. Tell him to go and caress his wife," Nandipha's hair spoke to her, outside of his hearing. She ignored it. She planted her hands at her sides, staring at his broad nose to avoid eye contact.

"No, I am not doing it!"

"Darling, I insist."

Her hair became wound up. "She said No. No means no."

Nandipha huffed. "No!"

Abruptly, and with impatience, he removed his hand, turned around, and went back to where he was standing, with his back to her. A set of footsteps approached from behind. Nandipha jumped, startled. There was a man, but she couldn't get a good look before he pushed her shoulder forward, keeping her facing in the direction of the tents and Andries. The man shoved a pistol at the nape of her head and slanted it toward her brain.

"Do not worry, Dipha. You may not be able to see his face, but I can see him just fine. He does not deserve to be living. The first chance I get, he will die."

Nandipha gasped, her eyes beaming into Andries' back.

"How dare you?" Nandipha and her hair both knew if they tried to turn around and toss him to the skies like they wanted, the gunman would shoot first. It was either save Andries' enemies or save themselves. Nandipha would sacrifice herself for all of their lives. Her hair felt like she had no choice. Protect Nandipha at all costs. The tresses upon her shoulders fluttered, growing and growing, making waves in the air like the ocean, until it reached the tents. Her hair had the added effect of not only growing but thickening, replicating to form stronger, vaster clusters of hair. One minute, the Baster tribe was sleeping, the next minute, they were awakened by a dark shadow of sudden pressure and extreme weight. Their eyes shot open but they couldn't scream. She hated to hear the screams; all they could do was stare at this dark and disembodied figure as it hovered over their faces and flattened their bodies. To no avail, they sought wiggling to escape. Unable to fight, they were paralyzed and suffocated by the hair. She pressed down on them until their bones splintered and cracked until blood spewed from every orifice on their body. They were crushed, splattering skin and end trails everywhere, hundreds of them at a time.

Rain clouds formed thickly over the village where the wives and children of the warriors slept. The grass was derelict green. Awakened by incensed voices, Almara was greeted with goosebumps and a pit in her belly. Every day, since the day her father had left, the hole had grown larger. She slid off of her cot and kneeled at the opening of the hemispheric hut. Outside, the elders argued over whether they should go searching for answers. It had been days since the infantry were expected to return from battle. Many of the wives were in denial, but deep down, they knew the truth. Almara was twelve and although she begged to be taken with them, she was told to stay behind. A couple of dozen men and women saddled up with horses, donkeys, and a covered wagon. They would travel for three days and three nights before reaching Griqualand West. As they said their goodbyes, Almara, known throughout the village for her nimble ways and quiet footsteps, climbed into the wagon and hid under a pile of covers; no one noticed, distracted as they were, exchanging goodbyes, handing out parcels of food, and ensuring the men would be protected on their journey. Almara's parents were with the missing crew.

Their nomadic tribe called themselves the Bergenaar Basters. In the weeks prior, they had sent a thousand warriors in response to the execution of six Bergenaar chieftains, to retrieve stolen cattle and take down the man responsible for it all. The most calculating Black man in a 600-mile radius of Griqualand West, South Africa: Andries Waterboer. The journey felt long and tiresome for Almara, who was only twelve years of age and could not help but be rattled with worry. She was found only hours after they left the village, curled up in the corner of the carriage, her thin nightgown barely keeping her warm, as they moved closer and closer toward Griqualand West. It was one of the women looking for the parcels of food that found her, and quickly scooped her up into her arms when she did, comforting her the rest of the way there. She knew Almara's life would never be the same again once they reached the camp. When Almara and the other Basters arrived, what they saw was indistinguishable from one person to the next. The smell was unholy, and there were no bodies to bury. It was a massacre, and their only option was a mass funeral. The only living creatures around were vultures, looking for scraps of flesh. They ran for fresh air, but the stench followed. They could taste the copper-iron smell of blood, like putting chicken and beans in a bag and leaving it outside for weeks during the summer heat to decompose, to rot, to fester. Then opening the bag to mix in some food-poisoning diarrhea and the strongest catfish stink bait you could find. All of that in a dumpster, with the fresh puke. That was the smell. The sight couldn't be wiped from their memories with hypnosis. They burned the entire battlefield.

Falsehoods about Nandipha's intentions were spread by Andries for added intimidation: Anyone in his circle should be feared the same as he. Rumors that the few Basters that tried to run were dragged back in, that the mistress bragged about her hair binding them at the ankles and pulling them away from freedom. Lies about how she covered their mouths to silence the squeals and suffocate them slowly. When they arrived, Almara stared, unblinking. The pit in her stomach had lodged itself in her throat, and the woman that had been comforting her was now wailing beside her, like a folded piece of cloth on the floor, crumpled. Almara would never refer to herself as a Baster again. It sounded like the word bastard, it came from the word bastard, and unfortunately, she was one. She hated the word, to her, it meant mutt. Without her parents, she was sent to live with her mother's family, because her father's side would never accept her. Without a home, she felt like a burden and an outcast, and she wondered how things might have been, had she been born to parents that were both white, or both black. She wouldn't have to wonder too long.

18
TWO-TONE

The day I was tested was uncharacteristically arid. In South Africa, summer starts in December, so it was one of the hottest days of the year. Waiting on the Coloured-only bus in Cape Town, I sat reading a book. I was holding it in my left hand, clinching a folding fan to shield the sun with my right. I wore a sage sundress and sat upright with great posture. My legs were crossed at the ankles. I didn't want anyone to question my social etiquette. My face was covered in freckles and my hair was long and springy, a reddish-orange color. Unbeknownst to me, a white woman had walked up clutching her bag, assuming I would stand for her to sit. When I didn't move, the woman huffed, "Are you going to get up?" This was a damn good book I was reading and I was enthralled by the plot. I giggled at something as I read, unconsciously tuning her out. The lady stepped closer. She leaned in and said, "I didn't know kaffirs could read." Kaffir means nonbeliever. It was used to demean brown people during and after Apartheid. It's unbelievably offensive. Just know, it's referred to as the k-word in Africa, much like the n-word in the West. I was triggered. I stared into the woman's soul-lacked eyes. I gave her a once-over, taking note of her unstained and crisp white shirt, her long pleated lilac floral dress, and her ugly green shoes. Tacky. I left off right back where I started, into the woman's blue soulless eyes. I was tired of it. Tired of being treated like an animal, and the amount of time I'd had to deal with them had seemed even longer because of my age, despite how I appeared. I was angry because I'd done everything possible to ensure I wouldn't be called a kaffir, or even considered Black for half a second. My blood boiled and the anger migrated to my fingers. I wanted to run my hand across the seven seas of Europe and light the woman's face up with the vengeance of three furies. That was until the whites-only bus pulled up, to save me from a mistake that was to be worse than the fate I was about to be served—the pencil test.

The pencil test was one of the many tools used in South Africa to oppress brown people. I know, how could stationery oppress someone? Among a few other tests that could check our jawlines or ass size, the pencil test was used to categorize a person as Coloured, African, or European. Mixed people were considered Coloured, Black people were African, and white people were European. A pencil would be inserted into your hair, and if it fell to the ground, you passed. That meant you were white. If it stayed, then you failed and were considered Coloured. For Black people who wanted to change their race, yes, that was an option. They had the extra step of shaking their heads, and if the pencil stayed, they stayed Black. If it fell out, they could be reclassified as Coloured with the benefit of being treated better. Black people were at the bottom of the totem pole, even though Coloured people were considered criminals. It was illegal to have a mixed-race baby born to white and Black parents, but not illegal to have a mixed-race baby born to two mixed-race parents. Ass-backward. White people could be pencil tested too. Some were. If they were reclassified to a brown race, they were kicked out of school, shunned by family, and even a blood test couldn't revert the test results. Asians with straight hair were honorary white, but only if the moon of their fingernails were more white than dusty mauve. The white woman at the bus stop demanded a test on me, and when a white person demanded something, it was to be done, and it was to be done now. Right here, right now, at the bus stop. The bus driver shouted to the riders:

"Which of you nice folks have a pencil on you?" A white man eagerly walked to the front, slightly bent over to avoid hitting his head on the pulleys. He carried the pencil in front of him, letting it lead the way. "Here you go. I don't want it back."

The driver grabbed the pencil. As he stood, his belly held the wheel for support. Pants busting at the seams, he stepped out. The white woman moved aside, still clutching her bag. Her lips were puckered and pressed tight, she had something to prove. I continued to sit on the bench. The driver gave me a look.

"Come on now. Don't make me have to walk over there or it'll be more than a pencil you get today." I stood up, looking at the sky, thinking, *Lord please let this pencil fall out of my hair.* The driver held the pencil like a pocket knife that he was about to jab into my side. As I approached him, he lifted his arm and angled the pencil down, forcing it into my roots. I held my breath, and closed my eyes, waiting to hear the pencil hit the ground. When it didn't, I shook my head. It still didn't fall out, so I shook it harder until I became dizzy. I shook it so hard that I thought I might have brain damage. My hair was dry that day. As I said, it was arid. So, my curls were tight.

"Give me your passbook." He held out his hand. I thought, *why call it a passbook when it should really be called a fail-book? No matter how this test goes, I still lose because I'm part Black.* I was reassigned to Black. My worst nightmare. I was a Black woman, and I had a power. I wondered if I was evil. Was this my lot all along? Is this how Waterboer's mistress turned evil? I refused to endure more years of mistreatment. So, after that day, I decided I would leave for America. My thinking was that it would be better here. Segregation had just ended with Jim Crow, while Apartheid had no clear ending in sight. The only light at the end of the tunnel was white America. When I got to Atlanta, the southern hospitality was magnetic, in the beginning. Everyone greeted everyone. I hadn't fit in anywhere before. I was too Black for home, not Black enough for family, and too white to make brown friends. At least in Atlanta I could be myself, or so I thought.

One sunny Monday morning I went for a job interview at a five-story clothing store downtown on Broad Street, it had an escalator and a parking deck. I bought new stockings and wore my best dress. It was white and I wore some faux pearl earrings to match. I sat down amongst two other applicants waiting to be interviewed. The room had a damp smell to it, but the light that filtered in through the large white windows put me in a good mood, the way it danced across the table and the feet of the other women sitting across from me. It reminded me of the stories my mother would tell me as a child, when she would make shapes on the walls, using the light of the sun to make the shadow of her fingers stretch into little figures. One of the other women waiting was mahogany brown, with clear skin and her hair styled in a French roll with a cute hump in the front. She wore a double-breasted peacoat, black stockings, and her pencil dress peeked through the coat as she sat. Her gloves were worn, and off-white in color. She sat prissy, with her hands crossed in her lap. The other woman was skinny, dark-skinned, with beautiful hazel eyes and an elegant beehive up-do. Her coat sat in a chair next to her, so her mostly hunter green paisley midi dress could be seen. Tight in the waist with a crew neck, she stood out. When I came in, they had stopped chatting immediately. They looked me up and down as I had done the white lady at the bus stop. Now all three of us sat apart, me over here, them over there. They whispered too quietly for me to hear what they were saying, but I felt their eyes glance over me more than once. I watched the light dance across their feet, waiting for the interviewer to come out. A short lady with a slight hunch, pasty wrinkled hands, and a saggy neck came from the back. She abruptly stopped and looked at us all. Within seconds, she flicked her hand at the two Black women and said, "We don't need you two."

They looked at me and rolled their eyes as if I had done something wrong. She then pointed at me and said, "Come with me." I was hired on the spot. Days later, whilst folding clothes near the back of the store, those same two women came by for some stockings.

"I'll go broke buying stockings. They always rip," the prissy one said to the skinny one. I recognized their voices but didn't look in their direction. I kept my head down so I wouldn't be noticed, but they felt my energy. The skinny one nudged the other with her elbow, "Look." They walked near me, "I see you got the job. No surprise, though. You high-yellow bitches are taking all the good jobs," said the skinny one.

I took a deep breath to calm myself and kept folding. The prissy one added, "I don't know why they hired a mutt. If they wanted a dog, I could have brought mine. Maybe then I'd have money to afford new stockings."

19
THIRSTY

June 25, 2020

Brynn blasted the music so she couldn't hear herself think. She was listening to her favorite rapper, Gucci Mane, she played his songs the most and on repeat. She rapped the lyrics word for word, bobbing her head and pointing at the air. If she wanted to, the girl could create a language using his lyrics alone. She thought she was a gangsta in the car, but she looked like an angry kitten. Why do pretty girls love trap music? In the midst of her enjoyment, her phone rang. It was the doctor's office again. "You should answer that." Words of wisdom went to waste, as usual. She ignored it... Again. I'll call them back later. I've seen her in denial before, but never like this. The phone dinged with a new voicemail. Sitting at a red light, she saw blue lights ahead and went from rapping, singing, and smiling to a straight face. Maybe it was fear. Maybe it was anger. Maybe it was that thing she did when she pretended to be invisible. Either way, she wouldn't let the green-eyed, blue-blooded monsters see her smiling because misery loves company. They couldn't stand to see us happy, and she wasn't trying to get pulled over or shot dead for it.

There were at least four squad cars and the officers were handcuffing a Black man. *I wonder why they need so many police for one person.* Maybe they thought more Black men would pop out of the car like clowns, 15-deep? As we rode by, she acted like she was watching the road but she was side-eye staring at the police, making sure they weren't up to no good. It made her think of Cory. *Why did I have to be asleep? Did they gang up on Cory like that? Ugh, fucking evil ass motherfuckers.* Her phone dinged. It was a text from Marc, she ignored it and kept driving. *And this motherfucker here. It's been a month. What the fuck could he want all of a sudden? You know what? It doesn't matter. I'm going home. I need a hot bath and a glass of wine... Alone... In silence... And I'm going to watch what I want to watch. Fuck that nigga.*

"Brynn! Shut up!" I yelled to no gain.

I wish Cory were here. He would have known what to do when I was at the protest. He would have understood what I was going through and supported me. He would have been there for me.

"Brynn! Shut up!" I yelled again, but it was my survival instincts. She was zoned out. *I know I shouldn't, but I do miss Marc. I mean, how could I not? We were together for two years. I can't help how I feel.*

"Brynn! Red light! Stop!" Damn it, what was the point of my existence? Finally, she noticed the red light as she glided through it. She hit the brake, sliding into the side of a vehicle, bumping it on the driver-side. The Jeep floated to the other side of the road and stopped, the driver didn't get out. Brynn sat in her car, staring at the steering wheel as she whispered, "Oh shit, oh shit. Should I go check on them? I barely hit 'em. They should be fine." She rushed over, noticing the person inside taking off their seatbelt. He had hickory brown skin, a thick manicured beard, and some luxurious eyebrows. It was as if they shined.

"Did you not see me?" He asked.

"Did I not see you?" She cocked her neck back. "Did you not see me?"

"Yeh, I saw you as you run that light and drove into the side of my Jeep." He paused for a second, opening the door to give her a once-over. "Hold on... I know you."

"I doubt it," she said, stepping back.

"Yeh. We went to high school together. You went to Therrell. Your name is Brynn, right?"

He stepped out of the Jeep. Her gaze shifted upwards once he stood before her. Salivating over his biceps, she stuttered, "I don't remember you."

She was a dime magnet. He was fine as hell, and I bet he went to LA Fitness. That's where all fine men were born. I wondered why she was playing hard to get. After Marc, she deserved some eye candy. I would've been messy sex hair for him.

"You're still just as beautiful as I remember—a queen amongst wenches. I'm glad we crossed paths," he said, fixing his eyes on hers.

"Look at God. She ran right into you." I had to insert myself somewhere. Brynn giggled, blushing.

"Your smile is still as gorgeous as I remember." He turned around, reaching in the window for his phone. "Let me call you sometime."

"You cute or whatever, but I got a boyfriend. It was nice seeing—" She tried to walk off but was interrupted by his cold laughter.

"What's that got to do with me?" He asked.

"Nothing, I—"

"She said no, witcho thirsty ass."

"Exactly." He responded to Brynn, stepping closer. He grabbed her hand, cupping Brynn's four fingers gently. "Give a nigga a chance. Damn, I've been wanting to get at you since high school. What's up?"

She shook her head, smirking but flattered. She used the hand he grabbed to pull out her phone. "What's the number?"

"404-099-2697. Save me as Nardo."

How was he dictating how she should save him on her phone? "Controlling much? If it were me, I would save him as Master Interrupter with one word in the notes section, 'NO.'"

"As opposed to?" She asked because obviously, he preferred this nickname over his real name.

"You really don't remember me? You don't remember my name?"

She hit save, then looked over the phone at him. "No. What is it?"

"I'll tell you tomorrow when you text me." He reached out for a hug.

She reluctantly hugged him for sympathy because her next question was, "Aren't you going to call the police for a report?"

"Don't worry about it. I'll say it was a hit-and-run. You're good."

"That's illegal."

"So is running a red light." He winked. "Holla at me later."

We got back in the car and left, heading to a one-story building with a small red sign that read 'Package Store.' Brynn didn't go to the liquor store often, usually, she kept a big bottle of vodka in the cabinet for those days when she needed a little numbing. Today was different. White liquor did the trick, but nothing like some brown for the blues. Not remembering the past couple of weeks when you wake up after a night of drinking is invaluable. I'm surprised it took her this long. As she entered, a weird feeling crept over her. She got goosebumps, and her stomach tightened. It was like she could sense trouble, but there were only a handful of people in there. The store layout was open, with tall shelves on the walls and makeshift aisles of liquor in the middle. The bright yellow lights flickered overhead and the air conditioning made the whole place colder than a freezer. She walked past a thin man with loose clothes, his shirt was torn at the neckline and he had dingy grey hair, it was balding in parts. He stood in front of the beer motionless. His hand was on the handle, but he was not opening the glass door. I thought maybe he was so drunk that he forgot where he was. But that wasn't it. In the door's reflection, Brynn recognized his face. She recognized his tormented eyes. Those butterscotch brown eyes. She was nervous, excited even. She hadn't seen him since the day her mother died. I thought she might try to get his attention. So, I gently touched his shoulder to make sure he didn't snatch back as they always do. She grabbed his hand, hoping he would turn toward her. When he did, she squealed,

"Dad?"

His upper lip twitched on the left and he cleared his throat,

"I see you've inherited your mother's... Abilities," his voice was raspy. She threw her entire body on him for a hug, squeezing him tight. The stench of liquor seeped through his pores. His arms dangled lifelessly beside him. She let go and stepped back, trying to ignore the faint smell of urine, too.

"What are you doing here?"

"Same thing as everyone else."

"It's been so long, years. I thought I would never see you again. Where have you been? What have you been doing?"

"What kind of question is that? He's homeless. What do you think he's been doing? Catching up on all the new TV shows? Hanging out with friends? Playing badminton? He's in survival mode."

The streets had gifted him with a long scar across his face that twitched like a worm when he spoke. "Surviving," he responded indifferently. Yep, I knew that was coming.

"I think about you all the time. Do you need anything? Where are you staying? GG is having a BBQ for the 4th. Maybe, you could come?"

He held up his hand. "Hey, look, I don't need handouts. I need to get a bottle so I can go," he held up a bottle of E&J at her eye level, blocking himself from her view.

"Are you riding the bus? I can take you home." She insisted.

He sucked his teeth, "what home? You've taken enough."

Her eyes squinted, "Dad, what do you mean?"

"Stop calling me that. I'm not your dad. I'm not your father. He's dead."

Her head tilted, "What are you talking about? Let me help you."

"You?" He pointed at her. "Help me?" He pointed at himself, the scar on his face writhed. "Are you going back in time to bring my wife back? Are you going to stop being a little brat and grow up?" He stepped to the side. "Move, kid."

He left her there, dumbfounded, wondering, "How could you treat your flesh and blood like this? Your daughter." We watched as he slammed the bottle on the counter and snatched a bunch of balled-up dollar bills out of his pocket to pay before he headed toward the door as if she was invisible.

She said it again, "Dad!," she cried.

He walked out of the store as if he heard nothing. She grabbed a bottle from the shelf. That's when I realized that the erk n' jerk didn't fall too far from the tree.

We drove back in silence, and at home, she listened to her voicemail: "This message is for Brynn Brown. This is Dr. McIntosh. I've tried reaching out to you a couple of times. Call me back as soon as possible. Thank you." She sighed and the figures in the paintings watched her as she peeled off her jacket and pulled out the bottle of liquor, pouring herself a glass. She ran herself a bubble bath, hoping to soak the pain away, but she couldn't help but replay the conversation with her dad. It ate at her, irked her, it jerked at her heart. She wondered if he loved her. If he ever loved her. Instead of having a shoulder to cry on, her tears helped fill the bathtub, and the liquor cheered her up. Eventually, the pain was drowning away, but the anger was floating on up. She grabbed her phone, thumbing through the text messages.

"Oops, I forgot Marc texted." She said sarcastically, shrugging her shoulders. Intoxicated, infuriated, and tearing up, her eyes were blurry. She started to type, "Why are you blowing up my phone? You didn't pay me any attention when we were together. Now that I've called it quits, you want to treat me like I exist. Well, you can call your little bitches. Don't call me. Don't text me. Do you."

Send.

"That wasn't Marc you were texting." She breathed a sigh of relief, leaning back into the tub, the nape of her neck saturated with water, even I was starting to relax. Brynn thought she heard a whisper but ignored it. Something in the back of her head was telling her to look at her phone. Oh, it was me. There was something going on where sometimes she could hear faint whispers of my voice. I hadn't figured out the similarity yet. She wiped the tears from her eyes and pulled the screen closer to her face. "Oh fuck." She threw the phone on the rug and it swallowed it.

"I thought that said, Marc. That says, Nard. What happened to the 'o' in Nardo? Why did I listen to him anyway?" She goes on mocking a deep voice, "Save me as Nardo."

"Idiot. I shouldn't have saved you at all," the water splashed from her hitting it. I know why she listened to him and left off the 'o.' She was distracted by his sexy bawdy. The phone dinged. She looked up at the ceiling and took another sip of liquor, sinking deeper into the tub.

"This man is going to think I'm crazy. I must be since I'm drunk texting. Who does that? I can't look at the phone. I can't do it." I thought she was overreacting. "It wasn't like you sent a pic of your twat. Relax." She thought she heard whispering again.

"Okay, I'm seriously losing my shit..." She looked up at the bathroom window above the tub but it said nothing, "It's probably just folks talking outside."

Could she hear me?

20

HAIR OF THE DOG THAT BIT YOU

June 26, 2020

In the morning, she sat cross-legged on the couch and turned on the TV for some background noise. A theatrical trailer began playing, "Coming this summer, Cthulu. Part man, part octopus. All destruction. The Universe has no chance. See it in IMAX and 3D." The pronunciation of that was interesting. Kuh-thoo-loo. I liked it. He ain't just got these hands, he got these tentacles.

Deciding to read Nardo's message finally, Brynn took a deep breath, opened her eyes and checked her phone:

"So you don't have a boyfriend?" Bursting into laughter and smiling, she texted him back.

Brynn: It would seem that way.

Nardo: When you lettin' me take you on a date then?

Brynn: First, tell me your real name.

Nardo: I don't like my name. Just call me Nardo.

Brynn: Okay, I'll call you 'No Date Nardo'.

Nardo: You funny. It's Lennard.

Brynn: Ok Lennard. I'm free next weekend.

Nardo: That's too far. Let's go tonight.

Brynn: What's the rush?

Nardo: Nun. I just know a good thing when I see it.

Brynn: Sure, you do. Where you trying to go?

Nardo: Just be ready at 7 and send me your address.

Brynn: Kk.

Nardo: Don't type that. It looks too close to KKK.

Brynn: You thinking too hard.

Nardo: I thought men didn't think. I'm not like the dudes you used to.

Brynn: We'll see. ttys

She figured, why not go out with him? It would be a good distraction from the fuckening, and you know what they say, the best way to get over someone is to get under someone else. *Oh shit! With everything going on, I forgot to call the doctor back. What am I going to do if she says it's bad? If I'm dying, I'd rather not know right now. I don't have the bandwidth. If it's fibroids, then I can't perm anymore. I need my hair done, though.* The line rang. Brynn was transferred to the doctor. She was squeezing her fingers crossed for good luck.

"Hello, Dr. McIntosh speaking." She spoke fast.

"Hi. This is Brynn Brown. You left a voicemail for me to call about my test results. Sorry, it took so long to call back."

"Yeh. I have your file here." The doctor's pin clicked. "It's not cancer, but there's still the matter of the fibroids. We need to get those under control."

"So, I do have fibroids?" Brynn took a long blink and uncrossed her fingers.

"I was pretty confident, but we're sure now. I'm going to transfer you to the front desk. I want you to make an appointment for next month to discuss your options. Did you watch the documentaries I suggested?"

"Yes. They were enlightening. I think going natural is a smart move."

"Enlightening, huh? It's important that you consider the consequences of your actions, Brynn."

"I will. I mean, I have. I'm definitely going to do it. Thanks, Dr. McIntosh." Brynn threw her head back slightly in annoyance.

"Have a good day, Brynn."

Time flew by, but Brynn was ready at seven o'clock on the dot. She sat waiting for Lennard, who was unapologetically fifteen minutes late. He blamed his tardiness on an Asian woman driving too slowly. Even going the speed limit, a slow driver can't make you that late. He texted for her to come outside, which she immediately did. He arrived three minutes after the text without explanation, gesturing for her to get in. When he pulled up, she noticed the thin blue stripe on an American flag as the grill insert of his Jeep.

"Ew." She paused momentarily, thinking she should go back inside because she'd rather binge-watch Netflix than go on a date with a pig. As far as she was concerned, anybody representing the law was the enemy, but she decided to take the free dinner. What was the worst that could happen? She buckled up and sat her purse between her legs. He glanced at them, then reached over and touched her thigh. "That's a nice dress. Pink looks good on you, baby girl."

She slid her thigh over to pretend she was adjusting herself, but also so he would move his hand. "Thanks. Where are we headed?"

He answered, slightly irritated, "Just sit back and chill. You'll find out when we get there."

Damn, this man is good at not answering questions. Simple questions. Wonder what tactics he's going to pull out of his ass when I start asking the hard questions. She responded defensively, staring out of her window, "I'm just trying to make sure I'm dressed appropriately. Also, can you roll the windows up? It's hot."

Had he never dated a Black woman before? I was about to sprout roots up in that mug.

"You look good. You're thinking too much," he laughed, "ain't that what you told me?"

"Why are you being secretive? It's weird. You could be taking me somewhere to kill me."

"You're in the car now. How is knowing going to change that? I was trying to make it a surprise."

She huffed, *it ain't like he knows my favorite spots to eat. What do I need to be surprised for?* Looking up at the mini vest hanging from his rearview mirror, she concludes *he must really love his job.*

They reached the destination, and Brynn noticed a teal six-story fish stat-
ue that appeared to be coming out of the ground in front of the restaurant.
In her irritation, she chose not to speak. He expected her to be thrilled, ap-
preciative, delighted with joy, because this is not a restaurant that you take
a first date to. This is where you go on your wedding anniversary, or where
you celebrate Mother's Day. He wanted to make a grand gesture, but really
it was just a bold statement. That shit screamed small-dick energy. He was
doing too much—hard pass. They approached the hostess, and he mentioned
"Reservations for two under Lennard Westt."

"Good evening, Mr. Westt, with two-T's. Yes, I see you here. We'll have that
table ready for you in a few minutes." She responded.

He nodded, "Thanks, queen."

After about five minutes of waiting, Brynn finally spoke, "I hope we get a
booth."

He looked up from his phone, "Oh, you're done having an attitude?"

"You think I have an attitude because I got quiet for a while?" She snapped
back.

"I think we both know that when a woman is quiet, she's mad." He looked
back down at his phone, thumbs twiddling quickly.

"It could be that she was an introvert being introspective." Again, I was
unable to offer my opinion. Eventually they were seated at a table. A woman
approached in a black long-sleeved button-down shirt and beige pants. Her
strawberry blonde ponytail swayed behind her.

"Hi, my name is Mary. I'll be your server this evening. Can I start you off with
something to drink?"

"Yeh, we're ready to order too." Lennard pointed to the menu. "I'll have the
ribeye steak. Well done."

"Well done. That's blasphemy." Even as hair, I knew that.

He went on, "...and we'll both have a Coke." The server looked at Brynn for a few seconds, and Brynn nodded in agreement. "Uh, yeh. Okay, I'll have the Seafood Newburg. Thanks."

Now, if you're ordering a soda in Atlanta, Coca-Cola is the drink of choice. It's an unspoken law, but could a girl choose her drink or nah? *He didn't ask me what I wanted to drink, but maybe he was trying to be nice. Maybe that's what he thinks it means to be a gentleman.* She had an excuse for everybody. Most of the time.

"So, what year did you graduate from Therrell?" Brynn asked.

"The same year as you. I still can't believe you don't remember me. I played basketball. I was the point guard, number 10. Perfect ten." Lennard held his hands in the air beside himself like a champ.

"Oh okay," she looked past his arms at a table of people laughing at a distance. "I don't care for sports like that. Didn't go to the games either."

"Aw come on. You had to have went to at least one game."

"I went to a pep rally, but that's about it," she shrugged. "And that was only because it was during school hours."

"You missed out," he chuckled. "Aight. What you like doing then?"

"I mean... I like video games, Marvel movies, and I dabble in a bit of anime here and there."

"You a nerd, nerd."

Brynn blankly stared at him. Non-nerds usually use nerd as a bad word.

"It's all good. I ain't mad at it. I play a lil' GTA here and there."

Brynn wanted to change the subject. Talking about school sports and video games made her think of Cory, and thinking of Cory made her want to learn about the American flag on his Jeep, and whether this Lennard was like all the rest of them. Brynn asked, "Why do you have a bulletproof vest charm hanging from the rearview in your car?" He lifted an eyebrow for a second. "Oh, you mean the ballistic vest. I'm a superhero that can shrink. I use it to fight crime," he mocked. She got offended. "Avoiding questions again, I see. You must be in the military?"

"Not anymore." He shoved steak into his mouth. "I bleed blue." I would've bet he had a MAGA hat in the trunk to match that vest. "Wake up, Mister Westt."

Brynn looked up from her Seafood Newburg and stopped chewing. "Sorry, I was chewing. What did you say?"

"I'm not in the military anymore. I'm a police officer." Her whole mood changed. She shifted her knees slightly away from the table and her tone became dull. "Oh."

"What's that tone? My job's a problem too?"

"Four reasons," she said holding up a finger. "One, you were late." Two fingers, "you're a cop," three fingers, "you avoid questions," four fingers, "and four, you smack when you eat. Oh, and let me not forget how you touched my thigh in the car." One of his brows lifted, his lip curled, and his eyes squinted like he couldn't see. He paused taking in her impertinence. "What's wrong with being a police officer?"

She dropped her fork. "Seriously? Really? Does choosing to remain ignorant help you sleep at night?"

He slurped the bottom of his Coke. "I'm ignorant because I want to serve my community?"

"You're serving all right. Serving the white man's war with a side-handle stick," her eyes rolled.

"We put our life on the line to protect the lives of everyone else. So don't bad mouth police to me."

"You're fighting on the wrong side. When I see a Black cop, I wonder who comes first. His people or his partner? If a white cop had his knee on a man's neck and that man said he couldn't breathe, would the Black cop stop his partner or would he stand there too pusillanimous to intervene? I don't get how y'all sleep at night knowing you're betraying your own kind. Throw the whole human away."

"He was a rookie. Cut that man some slack."

"Who was?" She rested her elbow on the table, leaning her chin on her fist. She patiently waited for a response.

"Bruh!"

"I'm speaking hypothetically," she said.

"Sure, ok. I'ma let you have it, for now. I don't want to ruin the night, so let's move on."

Brynn accidentally caught eye contact with a nearby table, and they both quickly averted their attention to their food. Releasing the anger, she felt embarrassed but validated nonetheless. Her best friend was murdered by the police. Every one of them felt like the enemy. Lennard asked, "Are you going to tell me where you work? You look like a sexy-ass librarian or secretary. Just throw on some glasses. You got the look."

"Don't project your porn fantasies onto my Brynn."

"I'm focusing on school right now, but you can consider me an entrepreneur of sorts," she sipped her drink.

"Excuse me then, queen. Ms. Independent, don't need no man." She shook her head in disappointment, knowing he was speaking from a salty place. He went on, clueless, "One day, you can quit your job, and I'll take care of you. You ain't gotta work. That's a man's job." *He couldn't be serious,* she thought, *being taken care of does sound nice, but I'm not about to be barefoot and pregnant. Walking 'round this bitch cooking, cleaning, and sucking. I'll leave that one alone for now.* "Yep, every woman's dream." She rolled her eyes again after he looked down at his phone.

Why was it always the fine ones? They couldn't be smart and respectful gentlemen. There had to be something wrong with them, and it always snuck up on you too. The hotep, the self-proclaimed nice guy who believed women didn't want nice guys, the misogynist, the player, the mama's boy, etc. You would think their self-esteem would be high. Maybe that's the problem, it's too high. Their ego overflowed and their arrogance splashed onto other people. When they got to the car, Nardo turned on the music. Cee Lo Green – *Beautiful Skin* played. It's a subtle statement to Brynn that he thinks highly of her. For Brynn, it's a subtle statement that women should do as they're told or else. As they headed down HWY 75/85, Brynn saw a cluster of tents and hoped that everyone was alive and well. It wasn't called Hotlanta for no reason. The summer had been known to take a few lives, especially the homeless. She was distracted, so she didn't realize he was passing her exit, 20-East. She pointed at the sign. "I live in Kirkwood. Aye, where are you going? Take me home."

He pretended he wasn't paying attention but kept going on the same path. "Shoot, my bad. I go this way so much it's second nature." Though the sign was behind them, she still had her finger pointed at the windshield. "So, are you going to turn around then?" He turned on his blinker and got in the right lane. "You know what? I need to grab something from the crib real quick, and then I'll take you home."

He stayed on the highway until they got to Old National, made a left off the exit, and made a left onto Godby Rd. His house was a small gray ranch, a corner lot. The grass was patchy and the mailbox leaned on its side, I could tell he wasn't much for decorations or flowers. Lennard opened his car door, but Brynn didn't do the same. "I'll wait here."

He smirked, "Man, come on. I don't bite."

I was seeing red flags. "Ring the alarm. Drop a pin. Something. Nope, nope, and nope. This nigga finna kill us."

"Do you live by yourself?" she wanted to know if she was going to be gang-raped before the actual murder. "Sometimes," he sniggered. "You can sit on the couch. I just need to grab something from my room, and I'll be back in a second. Here's the remote."

What do I need with a remote if we're only going to be here a second, and why is it so dark? I know he doesn't call himself setting the mood because he's not getting any from me after tonight. Not at that cluster fuck of a date we had. Why am I even here?

She was too nice, that's why she was there. We should have knocked his ass out and taken the Jeep. This was kidnapping. This was unlawful imprisonment in the second degree. Brynn looked around the room, trying to pick up the vibe in all the darkness.

Yep, a man definitely decorated this place. Black curtains and a hand-me-down sofa. A black-background picture with a gold crown. I recognize that coffee table from IKEA and that TV stand too. That's about all he got right. He tried.

Bored, she got up and walked to a tall bookshelf in the corner of the room. She skimmed the books, most of which were about the Black man in America. She grabbed the first book that she touched. It was called, *Selected Writings and Speeches of Marcus Garvey* by Marcus Garvey. She read the back of the book, slowly sitting back down on the couch. She flipped through the pages, waiting for Nardo to return.

Suddenly, a noise came from behind her. Fap! Fap! Fap! She looked to the left and saw movement out of the corner of her eye. "What is that sound?" The sound continued. Fap! Fap! Fap! It sounded like claps. Small, continuous claps. Brynn turned around to see Nardo's pants on the ground. He used his left hand to lean against the couch and his right to jack off.

"Ugh, what are you doing?" She shrieked as she launched up from the sofa, tossing the book aside.

He removed his hand from the couch and stood up, allowing everything under his shadow to be seen. I knew it. "I fucking knew it was small. He shaved to make it look bigger. Hilarious."

Fap! Fap! Fap!

Brynn's mouth flung open, and she pointed at him with her whole hand cocked sideways, palm side up. "Really? Are you fucking serious right now?" He sneered, raising one side of his upper lip in disgust. He antagonistically bit his lip, staring into her eyes. He did everything to display his masculinity and manhood, but he didn't stop. Brynn was lost for words. She snatched her purse off the couch, grabbed the doorknob of the front door, inadvertently slinging a red, orange, and green African print dashiki to the floor. The door slammed shut behind her. He was a frigging bastard. No, really. Google it.

"Nasty bastard. Who does that?" She mouthed, opening the Lyft app. She sat on the sidewalk a street over, waiting for her ride. Her phone dinged. It was a text from Marc.

Marc: Hey

She stared at the phone, not knowing whether to say hey back, be rude, or ignore him. It was fine timing for sure. Sure, he was less of an asshole than Nardo, but still an asshole. Marc and Brynn had a history. She even missed him a bit.

Brynn: Wassup?

Marc: What you doing?

Brynn: Marc, what do you need?

Marc: I miss you.

Brynn: Ok.

Marc: Can I come through?

Brynn: I'm not home.

Marc: Cool. Tomorrow then.

Brynn: I have a hair appointment tomorrow. You can come Sunday.

"I know you said you missed him, but damn, you're going to let him come over without apologizing?"

DRY

June 27, 2020

B rynn woke up feeling dirty, violated, and in need of some TLC. "Good afternoon," Brynn greeted Almara. Almara turned around, looked at Brynn, then indicated toward the seat with her eyes. I noticed that today, they looked green. "Wait, does she wear contacts?"

Almara responded dryly. "Hey." Something was off. I could feel it in my roots. Brynn looked in her purse for a piece of candy, but only saw a Lemonhead. It reminded her of Cory. A pit grew in her stomach. "It feels like I haven't been here in months, but it's only been a few weeks since..." She hesitated and sat down.

Today day seemed like a struggle for Almara. She draped the cape around Brynn's neck with one arm and even though there was clearly something wrong with Almara, Brynn started a conversation anyway.

"You doing okay today?"

"I'm straight."

Brynn looked at Almara's shoulder through the mirror. Almara responded by spinning the chair around, so Brynn couldn't see the mirror. But I could still see.

"Can I ask you something?" Last night was still at the forefront of Brynn's mind.

"What's up?"

"You ever had a man pull out his... Member... Unsolicited?"

"Nah."

"Well I went on a date with this dude, and he took me to his house afterward, talking about he needed to grab something. I was sat on the couch and after a few minutes, I caught him masturbating behind me. It was so disrespectful. He made me feel like a walking piece of porn... Like my only use as a woman was to get him off. I'm like, was he going to nut in my hair? Rape me? It was so aggressive and violating. I had to leave in the dark and get a Lyft out of there. It's crazy, somebody could have grabbed me, I felt helpless. I can't stop thinking about how vulnerable I was. He was a damn police officer too. I can't imagine what it would be like to be with somebody like that."

Almara shuddered. "I hear you. That's foul."

Brynn had finally broken up with Marc as Almara had suggested many times before, and she didn't even notice. *That's foul*. That's all that was said, that was Almara's response? She was acting like she had a stick up her ass.

"I heard it rained at the protest. Don't look like your hair fared well." Almara went from being short to being an asshole. "Well, excuse us, your rudeness. We were trying to save someone." I didn't take kindly to insults. Brynn let it slide. Maybe Almara was having a bad day. "I had to go Almara. And it was a good thing I did, there was this woman there that got shot. Even though when I went for help, she disappeared, but still."

Almara grabbed a comb. "Maybe it was all in your head," she retorted, "people don't disappear, especially if they've been shot. I can't imagine someone walking around after being shot, no less disappearing." Now she was downplaying shit. Brynn chuckled. "True, but she reminded me of you actually." Brynn waited to see if Almara would interrupt with information. Almara's nose twitched. "How so?" She seemed worried.

"I can't quite put my finger on it. She had your aura or something. Maybe it was her voice." Brynn had a revelation. "I remember now. It was her perfume. Y'all wear the same perfume." Almara leaned over on the counter, facing the mirror. She must've forgotten that it was a mirror because her eyes got big like she swallowed a horse pill. That's when I knew. It was her at the protest. She's a damn shapeshifter, that cheeky bitch. That's why she's acting hurt. Her ass got shot. Of course, but I can't tell Brynn because she can't hear me. Brynn saw her from the corner of her eye but didn't turn her around.

"You good?" Brynn asked.

"Yep." Almara straightened up. "I was trying to remember what I'd done with my phone. I thought I left it in the car." She tapped her back pocket, "but, it's right here. I have it." She changed the subject, "I thought you said you were going natural after the protest? You can't heal and help folks if you're natural." Almara was losing it. Everyone could tell. Her pixie cut was slick back like she had been rushing, her clothes looked frumpy and most odd, she was off her game. *Who said anything about healing?* Brynn thought to herself. Almara dropped the comb and leaned over to pick it up, but she gripped her shoulder and winced in pain "Ouch! Fuck!"

Brynn turned around.

"You sure you're good? I don't think I've ever heard you curse like that. Let me get the comb. We can reschedule if you want." Almara snatched the comb, "I'm fine. Sit down." Brynn quietly sat. The eyes of the figures in the paintings kept moving, watching us from above. Almara started to shift uncontrollably, but it was subtle. Nobody seemed to notice but me. I was shocked. I wouldn't have guessed that the hairdresser was a shapeshifter. It happened at Almara's roots first. Roots recognize roots. She couldn't control her facial expressions and her eyes went from blue to hazel, then back to brown. It looked like she was glitching. Her face lit up with freckles and the skin around her cheeks got soft and droopy. Almara looked in the mirror at her hair getting curly. She shook her head, hoping to change back before anyone saw. She continued with her rant, "You know if you don't get relaxers anymore, you won't have your powers either." She sure was adamant about that perm. I wondered what she was hiding. And why? I knew it must be something since she was hiding the ability to shift. She was hiding who she was. Why didn't she want Brynn to know?

"Yeh. I know. Last time was going to be my last perm, but this time it is. I've made up my mind. I have to choose between my health or saving everyone else, and lately, I can't even do that, so what's the point?" Brynn said with dismay, holding up her right hand, palm upwards as if she were holding something invisible. "Save the world?" She held up her left hand with the palm up, "or save me?" Brynn acted like the decision wasn't difficult whilst Almara continued to persuade her, "I hear you, but having the ability to make a change, sacrifice for something, everyone doesn't get that chance." *Why is she trying so hard to convince me, and why does it seem to pain her?* Brynn finally found the nerve to ask, "what do you care?" Almara got annoyed, "I care because ain't nobody else out here trying to save us. We all we got." Almara glanced in the mirror again. Now her skin was a bit lighter. What an interesting turn of events. If only I could've told Brynn.

"I hear you, but I can't carry that burden anymore. The one person I wanted to save is gone. He's in a grave. All I can do is keep going. Living. Breathing. Being strong." Brynn said. Almara took a long blink and a deep breath.

"Why don't you do it?" Brynn asked.

"You know I can't."

"Well, aren't you helping others like you've helped me? That should be good enough."

Almara's face drooped on one side like she was having a stroke. She was angry and she couldn't control her emotions. She couldn't control herself. She was shifting again. Christine rushed over, I noticed her glancing our way after Almara dropped the comb, she must've noticed the glitching too.

"Almara, I think you're having a stroke or something. She gave Almara a look. You should come with me... to the back."

Brynn jumped out of her chair, allowing Almara the option to take hers. "A stroke? She should sit down."

"I'm fine," Almara quickly turned away as her face popped back into place. She rushed off with Christine. "Just give me a second. I'll be right back."

22
ELASTICITY

June 28, 2020

"You wore that hoodie to the store?" Brynn greeted Marc with concern as he entered her apartment. It hadn't been long since they got back together. Things still felt awkward between them.

He pulled the black hoodie over his head. "You saw me leave."

"Ain't it hot outside? It's dark too." She sprinkled seasoning salt on the broccoli.

"You know this Atlanta weather is bipolar. Gotta stay ready."

"Yeh, well, I want you to be safe too." She yanked at the oven door. "You know them folks out here looking for a reason. Any chance they get."

"I ain't changing me for them motherfuckah's." He stuck his hand between the couch cushions and moving pillows, the couch groaned under his weight. "Where's the remote?"

"It's right here, on the counter." Brynn flicked it forward. "What are you trying to watch?"

"OSPN." He flipped through the channels, stopping randomly if something caught his attention. "Look at this big-head fucker." He pointed at the TV.

Marc was always interrupting her peace, and I couldn't help but wonder where he found a mirror.

"I can't right now. I'm cooking."

He got to women's basketball on OSPN, but kept clicking the remote. Ah, there it is. The four men that talk about sports. They seemed engulfed in debate,

125

almost heated. How is this entertaining? Other than scrolling on his phone, watching anything sports-related seems to be his favorite pastime.

Brynn asked, "You hungry, Marc?"

"I can eat." He turned the volume up on the TV. "I'd prefer a drink."

"I'll make you a vodka and orange juice."

"Bet."

Multitasking, she put the lid on the rice, grabbed a bottle of vodka from the cabinet, and pulled the OJ out of the fridge. Of course, Brynn being Brynn, she had to put two ingredients in a shaker and Italian drinking glasses for good measure. She walked to the couch and handed him his drink. "Here you go, babe."

He grabbed it, not taking his eyes off the TV. He wasn't raised by wolves, a thank you would have sufficed. After a short while, he finished the drink and lifted the glass in the air, shaking the ice. Disgusted, Brynn asked, "Are you serious?"

"Let me get another one." He continued to shake the empty glass.

"You don't need another one. You have to be careful with your diabetes."

"You tellin' me like I ain't the one that got it?" He exclaimed. "Please, make me another drink." He asked, but it was more of a command than an ask. Brynn stomped off to the kitchen and snatched a dinner plate from the cabinet. She crashed it on the kitchen counter, adding baked chicken breast, steamed broccoli, and rice. It was piping hot with healthy portions. She marched over to the couch, standing between him and the TV, and pushed the dinner into his space.

His teeth smacked, "What's this?"

She moved the plate closer. "Food. You need to eat something." He took the plate, leaning to the side to see around her. She left and returned with a plate for herself. After they'd eaten, their dirty plates were stacked on the floor. Marc slid closer to Brynn, putting his head on her shoulder. It felt like some half-ass attempt to apologize. "Are you still my girlfriend?" He asked. What was he, twelve? "Yes." She looked at him, long enough to see him not looking at her. He started to caress her breast and his dick print poked through the sweatpants. She didn't take her eyes off the TV, even though she had no idea what the show hosts were talking about. Marc stuck his hand through the top of her shirt, pulling it down, messing up the elasticity, now it will never return to normal. She politely moved his arm. "You're pulling my shirt. Not right now. I'm tired. Let's watch TV."

"You don't like sports."

"I also said I'm tired."

"All you did was throw some food in the oven. It did the work for you."

"Next time, you do it then."

He waited a few moments and stuck his hand through the bottom of her shirt into her bra. He knew precisely where to touch to go to get her in the mood. He slinked to the floor and got on his knees between her legs. He grabbed both sides of her shorts, sliding them, and her panties, down to her ankles. He pulled them off and slid his hand up her thigh, caressing her clitoris with his thumb. He knew how to touch it. It was like he had more practice than she. He leaned inward for a taste and she sunk into the couch cushions, bracing herself with her hands. Touching him would be a waste. It would've inhibited her from imagining it was Cory. As she thought about his lips and his mesmerizing eyes, she moaned. She thought about those sculpted arms and imagined him biting that sexy ass soul patch. She thought back to their ride in the car, his hand on hers, his voice, his dimple. The hole in his face. The white sheet. The blood. Blood. "Stop, stop," she sat upright, pushing his head away. "I can't do this. Let's watch TV."

"What's wrong with you?"

"You!" I wish I could have told him.

"Did you hear that? Someone said something." Brynn looked around the room, then at the window.

"Now, you're hearing voices? Wow, if you don't want to fuck, say that." He picked up his phone. "It's all good."

"I said it twice." She got on her phone, too, eventually falling asleep with it in her hand. He nabbed it just as it was about to dim, heading to the text messages. Marc jumped up from the couch. "You fucking other niggas behind my back?" Brynn opened her eyes, looking at him standing over her. "Why are you yelling?"

"Who is this lame ass nigga?" He tossed the phone in her lap. She read the texts from last week with Lennard. "This is old."

"It's still June. How is that old?"

"You and I were broken up," she exclaimed.

"That shit don't count." He retorted.

"Exactly. It doesn't count toward this relationship because I was single. Anyway, you trying to tell me that you weren't with anybody that whole time? You know what, it doesn't matter because I'm not talking to him. I'm talking to you."

Everything she said went in one ear and out of the other. "You fucked him?" Marc asked.

"It's none of your business." She stood up and walked to the kitchen.

"So, you did?" He followed behind her.

"I don't need to answer you. We already had this discussion. And you ain't a saint."

"Fuck-you-mean?"

"You ain't innocent. The nerve of you to pretend you are."

"Did you fuck him?"

"Did you fuck 'em?"

Marc grabbed her by the arm. She pulled back in disbelief, and simultaneously, Marc's hand was around Brynn's throat. "What did you say, bitch?" Brynn's eyes got big. She was scared. Gripping Marc's right arm with both of her hands, she attempted to draw sympathy from what little conscience he had within him; she stared into his eyes with disappointment, hoping that would make him stop, but I knew he wouldn't. If she didn't leave him one day, he was going to kill her. He squeezed her throat tighter, turning his head to the side and leaning in, "I can't hear you." She gasped for words, trying to say stop, but only breath and stutters came out. As he slammed her into the refrigerator door, the impact made her ponytail slump, loosening me up for action. She didn't want to hurt him because he'd had too much hurt in his life. She wanted to give him a chance to be better, but he's had too many of those. The cereal boxes rattled angrily atop the fridge while magnets fell to her feet. That was my cue. If she wasn't going to fight, I had to do it for her. I reached out and extended my tresses. I wrapped around his wrist, altering his temperament and intimidating him with force. His grip loosened. "I'm sorry," he whispered. Brynn still held his arm with both hands, trying to breathe again. She let out a cough as she pushed his hand down, away from her neck, side-stepping in retreat. His arm flopped to his side like dead weight. He stood there like a pouting toddler, head hanging low, saying nothing. She wanted to believe he was sorry, but you can't believe a forced apology. She had no words for him. She was tired. Tired of his lies, tired of people being hurt, tired of trying to help people that couldn't be helped. She regretted having chosen Marc when the better man was right beside her the whole time. She missed Cory. He would have never put his hands on her in spite. She was tired.

Brynn straightened her ponytail. She picked up their dirty plates from the floor and rinsed them in the sink. She packed the chicken, rice, and broccoli in containers. She placed the fallen magnets back on the fridge. She was tired. In the bedroom, Marc was already lying, sulking in silence with a bruised ego, but that wasn't the only thing. Brynn lifted her chin and took a picture of her discolored neck with her phone. Thankfully, harder to see amongst brown skin, but the BBQ was soon approaching and GG didn't miss a thing.

Maybe it will heal by then. Damn, it'd be so much easier if I could just heal myself. I can't cover it and I never wear makeup. If someone asks, I guess I could say it was a hickey. No, that's doing too much. What if dad ended up coming? What would he think? Maybe I won't go to the BBQ at all.

Her thoughts were interrupted with solace. The soothing sounds of snores. It was music to her ears, for once. Brynn slipped into the sheets and picked up her phone from the nightstand, deleted the texts from Nardo, then hopped on social media. Perfect for feeding negative thoughts and insomnia. Let's get this algorithm on the road.

23
BUNS

July 4, 2020

BBQ is a cooking process. BBQ is a descriptor of cooked meat. BBQ is a form of entertainment. It's a vibe. Black people don't just do something, we become it, and we are it. Whatever it is becomes entwined in us, a representation of us. The BBQ was a culmination of our music, our food, our culture, and our drama –rolled up into an event spiced up with card games. It was a safe space where fake smiles and code-switching were unnecessary. There was going to be fake smiling, but it wasn't a requirement. Stepping into the BBQ was stepping into an alternate universe. All of yesterday's problems got put on hold. It was time to eat, gossip, and party. It was family time, friends time, and scouting time. Ain't no formal invitation to the BBQ, so there were cousins that Brynn didn't know existed and friends of the family that she was expected to remember from when she was five years old. Everybody and their mamma was there. The only requirement for the BBQ was to come hungry and stay all night but the start time was only a suggestion. The food wouldn't be done on time, and you'd better take a plate to go. Everyone came to the BBQ dressed in their Saturday best. It was like the first day of school. Everything Brynn did from the moment she woke up revolved around attending the BBQ.

The night before, Brynn had already picked out an off-the-shoulder baby pink floral sundress and hot pink thong sandals. It tapered at the waist and draped gracefully across her hips. She got her nails done and put me in a top-half bun. The back was half down, with loose curls pulled toward the front to hide the *Marc* on her neck. *Hide the scar, put on a smile, and keep it pushing. No one will notice.* Besides that little snafu, she understood the assignment. Brynn headed to GG's quaint house off S. Gordon St. in the SWATS, a predominately Black-owned neighborhood. Cars lined the street on both sides. The vibrations from the bass tingled her soul. Amongst them was a candy red 1985 Cutlass Supreme with suicide doors, a sinister dark green 1995 Chevy Impala SS with 30-inch DUB floaters, a broken-down Crown Victoria with the paint rubbed off, and a 2015 Phantom black Dodge Challenger. The ones that stood out the most had the deepest bass, the flashiest paint job, and the biggest rims. It wouldn't have been Atlanta otherwise.

A *Karen* lived across the street, you know because gentrification was becoming a thing. She was nosy as fuck, always looking to start shit. Her whole face couldn't be made out as she peeked through the blinds, but her blonde hair was like a bicycle reflector at dawn. I almost missed it, but suddenly it winked at me, catching my attention. I wondered why they were called fair. The motherfuckahs weren't fair, kind, or sweet. I changed my mind. They are fair. They're a fair of animals and a shitshow of clowns.

Brynn approached the house through the carport with a small packaging box in her hands. The glass jars inside clanked against each other. She opened the screen door. GG didn't like to use the front door, I couldn't figure out why. Maybe it's a habit passed down from slavery. That, or she didn't want folks to mess up her living room, tracking in dirt and 'outside,' as the old folks said. It was the first room you get to when you come in, the living room was her pride and joy, her baby. Back in the day, she used to have plastic on the furniture, and none of the kids were allowed to go in there. She's a bit more relaxed with those kinds of things these days.

Brynn placed the box on a circular kitchen table. It wobbled a little because the twisty thing at the bottom of one of the legs had been missing for years, or it had run away and never thought to come back. Brynn walked forward to the den. She stopped near a single-seat recliner that GG sat in. Brynn waved at the few people chilling on the couch. A cousin, a neighbor, and a man she'd never met. She then leaned over to give GG a cheek kiss. With the grace only of a grandmother, GG gently pulled Brynn's face into her cheek to accept the love—a show of appreciation. "You got my chow-chow?" GG whispered near Brynn's ear. Brynn smiled charmingly and pointed at the table behind her.

Back in the kitchen, Auntie Casey was zipping around like she had super speed. She was at the oven checking the mac-n-cheese. Next, she was cutting onions for the hamburgers and hotdogs, and then she was at the sink rinsing off a green pepper. Auntie had a young spirit and despite her aging soul, she was in good shape. She was the definition of "black don't crack". Her complexion was on the lighter end of the brown spectrum but I wouldn't consider her to be light-skinned. I only know her age because of the veins in her hands, her wide booty, and the slight bags under her eyes that she tried to cover with makeup, even though that was a shade lighter than it should've been.

"Hey, Brynn. I didn't see you come in. How are you doing, baby? Would you grab that bowl of eggs and cut them up for the potato salad?" All of these were rhetorical questions. Just part of the greeting. Brynn grabbed the bowl. "Yep, I got you." She opened a squeaky drawer next to the fridge for a small knife and began cutting the eggs. "Do you want me to put the relish in, too?" This time, Auntie opened the drawer and grabbed a big spoon. She replied, "Go ahead, but don't be shy with it. Get heavy-handed." Brynn scooped the relish in, and before she knew it, the jar was empty. When she was done, Auntie judgingly looked at the potato salad, then back at Brynn, then back down at the potato salad. She smiled. "That's perfect. Go say hey to your uncle before he sees you and brings his drunk ass in here, getting in my way." Brynn giggled. "Okay, but before I go, is that cornbread I smell?"

"Yeh, but you can't have none." Brynn leaned over to Auntie and whispered. "You trying to tell me that I can't eat my favorite auntie's cast iron cornbread? I'm eating alluhdat."

"I haven't seen you in months," Auntie smirked, half-serious, half-joking with Brynn for wanting something of hers without providing something in return. Time. "It'll be done soon. Now, get out my kitchen. Go speak to your uncle. He's in the back on the grill." It wasn't actually her kitchen, but whoever's cooking is who the kitchen belongs to. In the backyard, the sweet smell of smoke and char from the grill was foreplay to the nostrils. Brynn could almost taste the ribs. Some of her favorite artists blasted from the speakers: Outkast, Migos, Future, T.I., and of course, Gucci Mane, to name a few. Unc liked to control the music when he was on the grill. He said it helped him think. I would've loved some Cardi B, Megan Thee Stallion, Latto, and Lizzo thrown in the mix. Didn't look like Unc was doing much thinking, though, since he and the next-door neighbor were yapping about who was right, MLK or Malcolm X. I couldn't believe this was still a thing. The neighbor sipped his Miller Lite, "We need to work together to move forward," he said. Unc held the barbecue tongs, waving them all willy-nilly, "nah, young buck, you got it all wrong. By any means necessary." Unc had a haircut that reminded me of the stepdad from Bébé's Kids. He liked to wear white linen suits and Jesus sandals. I couldn't understand why anyone would BBQ with their feet out. Unc and the neighbor didn't notice Brynn, so she stood there for a while ear hustling. Maybe she would learn something. She looked around, trying to see whether he'd come or not, but he hadn't. Her dad was never gonna come, but she's Brynn, so she's hopeful.

"Hey, Unc. What's going on?" She finally interrupted before they got louder. Unc reached out for a church hug, greeting her, "Ain't nothing to it." Boomers had the weirdest way of saying hey. They both pretended they weren't just in a heated disagreement before she walked up, but she could tell that they were waiting for her to leave so they could continue. Whose kids are these running around the tables, screaming? The smell of loud ass perfume whacked Brynn in the face. It had notes of vanilla. Which reminded Brynn of cheap perfume. She hated that smell. *Vanilla should be an ingredient in a dessert, not an essential oil.* The closer the smell got, the more her nose burned. Brynn knew who it was before they spoke. She didn't need to turn around.

"Hey, Aunt Tina." Tina lifted her hand to wave but dropped it back down as Brynn turned to face her. "How did you know it was me?" Brynn had three aunts, having girls ran in the family. Her mom, Felice, was one of four. Aunt Tina was Mom's identical twin. From her healthy, long cookies-and-cream locs and those hazel eyes to her wide hips and thin waist, age looked good on her. Brynn thought about her mom when she saw Aunt Tina. She missed her mom. Brynn paused, thinking of how to respond.

Tina got closer. "You been avoiding me? I haven't seen you in forever. How you been?"

Brynn stared at her lips as she spoke. Looking into her eyes felt too much like home. "I'm doing good, busy with school and stuff." Tina knew Brynn was lying. "Well, you have to balance in life. Have to make time for family too." *That's why I'm at the BBQ,* but she couldn't say what she thought. "You're right, Aunt Tina. I'll work on that." Tina reached out with both arms for a hug. She squeezed tight like it would replace the years of hugs Brynn had missed from her mother, but Brynn quickly left without letting on that she wanted to escape. She made her way to a cousin that she hadn't seen in a while. He was playing cards, smelling re-dankulous. Tay gave no fucks. He stayed high. He did whatever he wanted. Once he saw Brynn, he stood up for a quick hug. "Cuzzo, what's crackin?" Even though she wasn't the baby of the family anymore, the family still treated her like she was. She liked the attention. It felt good to be taken care of, loved on, and treated like she mattered. It felt good not to have to take care of others for a day.

"Nothing much. I'm fine," she responded.

Tay sat back down at the card table. "Where's that lame nigga you always with?" Tay didn't like Brynn with Marc. He thought she could do better, but he slick respected him because they were alike. Fuck boys at the core. "I don't know where he at." Tay smacked his lips in doubt. She didn't want to go into it in front of everyone, and she definitely wasn't telling him about being choked because that might've sparked a manhunt. She vaguely added, "We broke up." Tay tilted his head sideways, hesitating for a second in skepticism and grinning, faking like he didn't know which card he was about to play. There was only one. He threw out the big Joker and said to her, "I'ma talk to you in a minute. I gotta take a leak." Just as she was about to continue making her rounds, she turned to see Marc staring at her from the sliding doors. He stood there like he got picked last in gym class. When he saw her see him, he waited for her to approach. Instead, she grabbed the closest chair to her and sat. She didn't have anything to say to him, and if she did, she wouldn't have said it there. Marc stood at the table where she was seated, but she didn't acknowledge his presence.

"You're not speaking to me?" He asked. She looked past him like he wasn't standing there. He sat down next to her. "I've been texting you, bae." *Don't call me bae now. I wasn't your bae when you had me hemmed up.* She looked down at her phone, "Yeah, I saw." Marc touched her hand and pulled it toward him. "You weren't going to reply? I only fight this hard because I love you."

I was both shocked and scared for him because, at this point, I could only stop myself so many times. *I thought you were sorry.* Before she could respond, we heard someone shouting. "12 outside talking 'bout a noise violation." A bunch of us headed to the front.

Grandma Georgia - May 28, 2020

Grass grew between the cobblestone cracks. People locked themselves inside their homes, refusing to come out. Children peeked around the sheets that were used as drapes, longing to play outside again. He strolled the town, garbed in black leather gloves, a long black trench coat, and a wide-brimmed leather hat. Untrustworthy as a false god, he claimed to heal victims by using phony cures and handing out drugs for profit. His presence alone foreboded death. The man carried a wooden cane, removing patients' clothing without the need to touch them, examining them in vain. He kept aromatic herbs to ward off evil smells and keep bad air at bay from contagious victims: Lavender and dried juniper berries, which were a favorite as they were thought to be homeopathic by some and to have magical powers by others. Either way, the herbs had a calming effect. Some say they smelled woody, reminiscent of cedar or gin. The most disturbing part of his getup was the mask, where he stored his herbs. It had a curved beak like a scavenger bird and circular glass openings for the eyes. It wasn't disturbing because he resembled the Grim Reaper, or that the mask looked like someone cut off a bird's face and wore it with pride, it was the fear behind the mask. That was the last thing victims saw before the pestis bacteria seeped out of their pores and their skin turned black as they were fatally necrotized. Seven hundred years ago, the Black Death stole lives, ravaged societies, and gave way to a deadlier force than itself, the plague doctor.

Handed down to me from my great-grandmother, I carried a cane steeped in spirits. It was made of wood with a black leather handle shaped like the plague doctor's mask. I kept herbs in the beak and took my cane everywhere with me, keeping it close even though I didn't really need it for walking. I guess I liked to lean on the memories for support. I arrived at the Dekalb County Jail. The waiting area was fairly large and wide open. It had no windows and circular pillars. In the middle, were hard blue chairs lined in rows. I hadn't been here in many years, but even in the morning, people were everywhere. A gang of officers was gathered near a side door of the jail, giggling and gossiping in packs like schoolboys. Families awaited the release of inmates. They seemed annoyed, drained, and impatient. They huffed and they puffed and they rubbed their heads. I tottered to the counter with extra emphasis on my cane. One person was there. A man with blonde hair and blue eyes sat behind the plexiglass with his feet propped on the desk. In an attempt to jog his memory and to learn what he knew, I told him, "I'm looking for my granddaughter." He looked up at me after a pause and said, "Get in line." I looked behind me because there was no line. And I wasn't getting in it or behind anyone else even if there were. Been there, done that. I wasn't moving. I didn't move. I gave him more details. "My granddaughter was brought in late last night. You might remember her –Black, 5'3, probably had on pink?" He brought his hand up to rub his chin. I noticed the tattoo of the Celtic cross on his inner arm. All in one motion, his feet dropped from the desk as he stood. It was very, how do I say this, soldiery.

"Come to think of it. There was some feisty little broad come in here yesterday. I heard she was starting shit. I can't let her out."

It took everything in me not to snap. But you got more with honey than vinegar. Besides, that comment was the confirmation I needed to get in his mind. I slid my leopard-patterned bonnet down the side of my head and into my tan pebble grain leather Dooney & Bourke purse. I'd forgotten to take it off rushing out of the house. He stared right at the black patch of hair living amongst my gray. The tips of my hair wiggled. If you had blinked you'd have missed it. As the words left his mouth, melanocytes left the tips of my hair and entered his eyes, like spiders, they were dark in color and dendritic in shape. Too small to see with the bare eye, too tiny to feel. He never saw it coming. As he spoke about Brynn, the memory of her faded. His memories were absorbed within my cane herbs to do with as I pleased. I would extract the memories and watch them like a movie, or do nothing with them at all. Either way, they were gone from his memory. Along with the thoughts I took, the words escaped his tongue.

"What was I saying?" He shook his head like a wet dog, trying to un-fog his brain. "It feels like I was looking through a kaleidoscope."

I responded, "I don't know, sweetie, but I just gave you bail money for Brynn Brown. You were releasing her." I didn't think that would work. Don't they keep track of these things on their computer machines? He looked at me suspiciously with his nose turned up, suddenly smelling a strong odor. "Ma'am, are you drunk?"

"No, dear. That's cologne you smell. My husband likes to wear it to bed. It has notes of cedar and–"

He grunted, interrupting me, "Brynn Brown, eh? Take a seat. She'll be out."

I wasn't married, but I had to lie so he wouldn't throw me in jail too. Back when I was dating, this sexy gentleman wore a cologne by the name of Aqua di Gio. It had notes of nutmeg, bergamot, and cedar with a woodsy finish. He used to go on and on about the notes in different colognes, but Aqua di Gio was his favorite. I guess his talkativeness came in handy. The cop sat back down and propped his feet up. I made my way to a chair next to a woman and her three daughters. They reminded me of my once little warriors –Casey, Felice, Faustina, and Kella. Casey always knew things she wasn't supposed to know. Sometimes, I thought she could see the future. Felice was strong-willed and stubborn. You could never change her mind. Faustina, or just Tina, was naturally supportive and always knew what to say, except when she and Felice were at each other's throats. I never knew twins could argue so much. The oldest of the four was Kella. She was emotional and downright difficult at times, my most challenging baby. She stayed out of trouble... For the most part. Too smart for her own good.

Kella left home as soon as she turned eighteen. She said she needed a change of scenery, and some independence, but it was to escape the family. To escape me. I think she felt like an outcast because she was the only one who didn't have rooted powers. The only one with a white father. She asked me if she could meet him, but I said he was not around. I never said where he was, that he was dead in the ground. How could I be honest when I killed him myself? He couldn't be trusted. What's that saying? The only white man you can trust is a dead white man. I thought back to the day Kella left. The twins were sixteen and Casey was fourteen. The girls stood outside of the house, watching as Kella carried her brown hard-shell luggage and threw it in the trunk of my teal 1987 Buick LeSabre. That car was like a boat, a smooth ride. I gestured toward Kella, talking to the three of them.

"Okay now, give your sister a hug, it'll probably be a while before you see her."

Felice angrily stumped over and loosely threw her hands around Kella. Tina put her arms around the both of them and squeezed, but Felice wasn't having it. She didn't want her sister to leave and she didn't want Tina touching her. She snatched her arms back and ran inside. Casey stayed in place. She mumbled something under her breath.

"What did you say?" I asked.

"Nothing," she sulked, closing her eyes.

Tina interceded, "Tell mama what you said, Casey."

"I said try not to get pregnant!"

"Hush. Why would you say that?" My eyes bulged. I gave Casey a soft shove on her shoulder, pushing her toward Kella.

Casey shrugged, looking down at the cracks in the driveway. She dragged her feet over to Kella, "Sorry, I just had a dream is all."

That day stuck with me because no more than six months later, Kella called to say she was pregnant, but that's a story for another time. I missed her, and rarely got to see her after that. It left a hole in her heart and it's why I put so much effort into making sure Brynn was well taken care of. That's why I got out of my comfortable bed to get her out of jail first thing this morning.

Later that night, I steeped the berries, alongside some cardamom pods, and extracted the memories into a gin for the added pleasure of a buzz. Of all the memories I've consumed in my life, some were mystifying. Some were blood-curdling, some were enlightening. Some memories turned to nightmares that would keep me up at night, swallowed memories stayed on rewind. But seeing things from the officer's perspective proved useless, other than learning of my granddaughter's potty mouth. My phone rang.

"Hey Ma. You got a sec?" Casey sounded worried.

"Yeh. What's going on, baby?"

"I had this dream and I feel like it means something. Like something bad is about to happen."

"Well, all we can do is wait and see. All your dreams don't come to pass. What was it about?"

The air was murky and thick, and Casey stood at the end of a cul-de-sac. It was nighttime and eerily quiet. Casey couldn't move, she said, she was speechless and fearing for her life. There were two snakes in the middle of the road. One had a burnt umber pigment with stripes of eggshell white that created a circular pattern around its body. It was curled up in a clump, not bothering her... Yet it seemed large enough to make a lasting effect had it decided to. The other was lawn green all over with yellow eyes. It didn't seem menacing, but a snake's a snake. They uncoiled themselves and slithered toward her, leaving imprints like shadows on the tarmac road. She stepped backward and a figure appeared. It was difficult to see in the thick air, it trotted with purpose, blending in with the darkness. It waddled in her direction, hefty and quick. It was a pale boar heading for the snakes like they had beef. They lifted their heads and drew back in defense. The boar got closer and the green snake threw its body toward it in an attempt to strike. It was life or death. The boar stomped and bit at the snake. The first snake struck back, but the boar got ahold of it and slung it across the street like a ragdoll. It tried to escape but was unsuccessful in every attempt. The boar scooped the second snake, the green snake, greedily into its mouth and it hung there helpless, trying to position its body to get free. It twisted and twirled, curled, and bent. It jerked its body about. The snake coiled up toward the boar's face and struck at its eye, but the boar had the advantage of size and ambuscade. It ran off into the darkness with its meal.

"Hmph," I thought for a moment. "It sounds like the boar is just a pig. Maybe someone you find to be dirty. And the snakes are just... Well, snakey motherfuckers."

"Ma, have you been drinking?"

That was the second time I had been asked that today. I chuckled, "You talking to me like I'm the child. You called my phone. Now, you questioning me. Try to relax. I think things will be fine."

"Ok, Mama. If you say so."

"I do. Bye, baby."

"Bye, Mama."

I didn't let on how much Casey's dream bothered me. I was good at that. It was true that all of her dreams didn't come to pass, but this definitely felt foreboding. I couldn't sleep. *Who were these snakes? Who was the boar? Was I the snake for killing Kella's father? Was I wrong for what I did? Was I the boar? What if Felice hadn't died that day? Was Brynn the boar? Memories slugged through my mind like traveling through swamp water. I felt the presence of death.*

July 4, 2020

Hearing about police murdering innocent men made her stir, but it didn't wake her. The memories of her mother and father had her toss and turn, but they didn't wake her either. The memory of the folks at Southern Peaks probably still trying to hunt her down felt distant. Brynn wasn't concerned much about what would come of it. She doesn't care if people come looking for her. She might want it a little, then she could take fewer guilt trips. Help a little less to help herself more. Hurting her is fine, she's ok with that because it offers a reprieve from the pain of their absence. It's like self-inflicted pain. The distraction is welcomed. Cory's murder, though. That jostled her sleep. The problem is hurting those close to her. They've been hurt enough. Losing those she cares about makes her feel trapped with only echoes as comfort. She might as well lie there and die. That kind of hurt makes a person cling to those around her, good or bad. It makes her want to protect and defend them. GG had burglar bars on the windows for safety, but what about the trouble outside? The police showed up, clouding the party with impending doom. A damsel in distress called on her blue-blooded knight in shining armor to rescue her from her feigned imprisonment. Here to save the day with his mighty sword, someone must be cut down.

Most of the guests were gathered out front near the mailbox. We gathered for solidarity and support should things go awry. It's one thing to harm us. It's another thing to get away with it. GG stood near the house at the top of the driveway, observing. Karrine was no longer peeking through the blinds. Her A-line bob was apparent outside. She griped at the officer, "I asked them nicely to turn the music down, but they didn't." Tay asked the group of us, "Did anybody talk to her before she came knocking on the door with this bullshit?" He waited for a zeptosecond for someone to answer. "You didn't ask us shit, Karen."

Everyone giggled. She rolled her eyes and got closer to him. "My name is Karrine, pronounced Kuh-Rin. Not Care-in." Tay approached her, cupping his ear in a playact effort to hear her better. Blue blood put his hand up and stood between them. He looked at Tay. "Calm down and stay back."

Blue Blood looked at Karrine. "Ma'am, you've asked them now. They will oblige and turn the music down."

Karrine spoke again. "Officer, aren't you going to take him to jail for harassing me?"

Tay walked in a circle and threw his hands in the air. "Is this bitch for real? How the fuck was I harassing you?" She looked at the cop, pointing at Tay, whining, "he came out of the house and started harassing me."

"I wasn't harassing you."

"I only wanted you to turn down your music," said Karrine.

Tay laughed. "It's a BBQ. Have you ever been to a BBQ before? Probably not. You're not invited."

"You're disrupting the peace. You almost hit me with the door," she yelled.

Tay taunted her. "Now you're just making up stuff, just like a Karen. How did I almost hit you, and the door swings inward?"

"You called me a Karen."

"You're acting like one by calling the police on a party."

Blue Blood finally spoke again, "Folks. Hey, hey, folks." He seemed calm, almost unconcerned.

"First of all, I didn't almost hit her." Tay interrupted the cop's thought.

"I understand that. Just relax," Blue Blood said.

Karrine whimpered, getting louder, "He came out of the house and started harassing me."

"I came out because I couldn't hear you. Everybody was talking behind me."

"You didn't have to come out of the fucking house."

"You didn't have to come in our yard, knocking on our door either."

Karrine cried, "You're a Black man approaching a white woman. I feel threatened in my own home."

"We're not in your house, delusional head-ass."

She turned around to see that she was no longer standing in the grass of her yard. She looked at the cop, crying, "he literally came after me."

"Are those tears real? Look at Karen, an actress and all. Unbelievable."

A neighbor stepped up, "he didn't almost hit you. You're lying. I was walking to the backyard when I saw him open the door. Go home."

Suddenly, Blue Blood looked in Brynn's direction. They glared at each other. She was Medusa and he was stone, like that godawful racist monument staring down at her from his high horse. A looming threat. There they were, those inbred eyes. I recognized his vapid face and his wretched spirit. He looked at Brynn with a menacing smirk. He shouted, still locking eyes with Brynn. "Hush, be quiet. The both of you. We have a bigger problem, and it's not the music."

He paused for a dramatic reveal. "It's the witch y'all are harboring." He pointed to Brynn who was standing in the grass behind everyone else. "I've got a BOLO with your face on it. Come on, let's go," he commanded. Be On the Lookout? I didn't believe it. He had to be lying. Besides that, she couldn't move. She was stuck. If he's anything like the cop who took her to jail, she'll never see the light of day again. Besides, those two cops probably know each other. The group looked at one another. "Is he talking to you... Is he talking to you?" He sneered at Brynn with those mismatched eyes. She hated him. I hated him. He murdered Cory. I could feel it in my roots. Marc intervened because he knew the blue blood was referring to Brynn. He offered himself.

"She's good where she's at."

"I see we got ourselves a superhero. You going to pull a cape out your ass too?" Marc asked, "What's the problem, Officer?"

Blue Blood objected, "I don't want you. I've had my fair share of your kind. I want the witch with the demon hair." Wow! The belligerent kind didn't only come with inbred eyes. It came with a careless tongue, too. So nice –I could have trashed it twice. Marc walked toward Blue Blood. "I'm sure you can take another."

"Don't make me laugh, son."

"I'm not your son."

Blue Blood looked at Brynn again. "So, you cared more about that other one. Not fighting so hard for this one, huh?" Marc looked at Brynn, disconcerted.

"Oh, she didn't tell you how she flung a few guys around to save him?"

Brynn mouthed, "No," shaking her head at Marc.

Blue blood threatened. "Don't make me have to come to you, little girl."

"You're not going to do shit," Marc responded.

"Do you see a body cam on me, boy? I do what the fuck I please." He tapped the gun on his side.

Brynn still hadn't moved. She juggled the pros and cons, wondering if Marc was going to risk his life for her. *Am I going to let him risk it? After all the shit he's done, he deserves to be standing there instead of me. I deserve to be saved.* Blue Blood rehashed the park. "It's like the man said. If you don't pay, someone has to." He pulled the gun out of its holster and aimed it at Marc. The group gasped and backed up into each other. I couldn't believe this blue blood had the arrant audacity to threaten a Black man in broad daylight in front of everyone, without backup. Either he had more clout than we were aware of, or he thought his life was worth the sacrifice to have one Black man erased.

"What? What man are you talking about?" Marc was confused.

"The man at the park. Keep up." Blue Blood was unhinged. The gun moved as he spoke. He paused. "Oh, she didn't tell you about that?" Marc's lips quivered. Brynn didn't want to save him, but she felt bound by duty. *I didn't get* a chance to save Cory. This is a chance to redeem myself. I can't let him die like this, but he put his hands on me. He choked me, and he could have killed me that day. I could be dead right now. I should let him die. I deserve to be free. Marc was caught in Blue Blood's crosshairs, but his aim wasn't only for Marc. It was for the people. Blue blood took a deep breath.

"Not in the saving mood today?" He asked Brynn.

She still hadn't moved, contemplating what to do. The blue lights on the squad car transported her back to the night Cory died. Her stomach twisted. She replayed the scream in her mind, the sheet, the blood, the hole. The pieces of Cory. The pieces of him that she would never get back. The pieces. That's when Tay walked over to Marc. He stood beside him and lifted his white tee, flashing the semi-automatic pistol in his pants. "You don't want no problems."

Blue Blood yelled, "Drop your weapon." His tone was serious now. "Get down on the ground!" He waited for a moment, but Tay yelled back, "you put your gun down. It was all fun and games when you were the only one with the power, huh?"

"I'll give you to the count of five, son." I wonder if he gave Cory until the count of five.

"One." He started counting. Brynn was still uncertain if she should intervene. I was sure that if we didn't, it would be mayhem. Behind Brynn, I was growing expeditiously. I was back length, waist length, and then calf-length until I was at her feet, touching the ground. I pulsated in an attempt to change the mood. Everyone's mood. That was impossible. I wasn't that strong.

"Two."

Erik caught a glance of me out the corner of his eye. He didn't know what I was doing, but from his experience, he likely didn't care to find out. I had to hurry. I had to get to them.

"Three."

Frantically, I bobbed and weaved through the people standing before Brynn, zig-zagging like a garden snake, dashing like a squid before it was too late. I'd never moved so fast.

"Four."

Tay grabbed the handle of his pistol and a shot rang out.

BANG! Marc was closest to me. I was frantic. There wasn't enough time. I flicked him on the shoulder to knock him out of the trajectory of the gun. If I hadn't, he might be dead. He fell into Tay.

BANG! Marc dropped to his knees. He made an ingressive hissing sound. The sound you make right before you cry out in pain. Blue blood jeered at Brynn, "Oh, you did the hard work for me, killer."

Brynn's feet still hadn't moved. She was fatigued. Everyone was startled. Mouths flung open. Eyes darted around. Whispers echoed. They nudged each other, shocked but unafraid of me. I'll bet they wondered what Brynn had become, secretly hoping she was about to kill this Blue Blood dead in the street. That's what I should have done. Showed him the same respect they show us. GG hurried to the end of the driveway, traversing the concrete, her cane click-clacking along. She removed two hand-carved wooden spiral chopsticks from her hair as she walked. Her tresses fell, softly hitting her shoulders. The tips of her hair swayed slightly as if the wind had blown. Her melanocytes attached to everyone outside –Tay, the group, and the neighbors. Everyone except Brynn and Marc, who were both weak and out of it, lying on the ground. The cop watched as everyone became confused. "What are we doing out front?" someone asked. The cop looked at Georgia, already knowing what Brynn was. Putting two and two together, he scurried to his car. GG tap-tap-tapped her cane on the ground,

"Everybody inside." In and out of consciousness, things were blurred, and with every blink, more time passed. We got glimpses as they loaded Marc onto an ambulance. We woke up after about fifteen minutes.

"Is he okay?"

Leaning on her cane, GG stood over Brynn in the grass, staring at the bruise that Marc had left on her neck. "Why did you do it?"

"I don't know. Huh?" Brynn leaned up on her elbow, discombobulated.

"You don't know?"

"Why did I do what, GG?" Brynn stood to gather herself, wiping the dirt from her sundress.

"Why did you save him?"

"Why did I save my boyfriend?" Brynn scrunched her face.

GG rebutted. "A friend at best. A boy, to say the least. He doesn't need saving." GG looked toward the end of the street as she heard police sirens from afar.

"He was trying to protect me," Brynn pleaded.

"And you couldn't even let him do that. If you had time to save him, he had time to save himself."

"He froze."

"Remember what I told you." GG moved the cane to her other hand. "It's you or them, life or death. Every fight ain't your fight."

"What about Cory? Are you saying I shouldn't feel guilty for not saving him? That was his fight too?"

"My granddaughter is not some human shield to be used for protecting grown-ass men."

"I couldn't watch another person I love lay on the ground, covered in a sheet, to be toted off on a gurney. It's not like I jumped in front of him. It was my... Hair." Brynn trailed off the last word so as not to be heard.

GG was interrupting anyway. "Look." She pointed at the blood on the ground. "What you tried to avoid is still happening."

Four squad cars pulled up. They turn off their sirens but leave on those blinding lights.

"At least he's not dead," Brynn emphasized.

"Yet." GG turned toward the house, throwing her hand in the air dismissively. "Sacrifices must be made."

"That's what I was trying to do."

"No!" GG furiously turned back. "You made a knee-jerk decision from a relentless need to control the situation. You aren't sacrificing. You're being sacrificed." Brynn stood dumbfounded. She couldn't wrap her head around the words, but she knew there was truth to them. Looking in the mirror is easy but swallowing the truth takes toil. GG went through the front door. Brynn stood by the gate to the backyard. The music had been cut off and the vibe was dead. She could hear folks saying their goodbyes. She didn't have to listen hard to hear Tay, he took over the conversation, indifferent to anyone's feelings.

"Okay, so am I crazy, or did anybody else start seeing shit just now?"

"I can barely remember anything for the past few minutes," someone added.

"Seeing shit like what, Tay?" Aunt Casey asked curiously.

Tay answered, "I don't know. Maybe I'm trippin."

The neighbor explained, "It was like I was looking through a kaleidoscope. Psychedelic as hell."

Tay laughed, "Who spiked the punch? I got a drug test on Monday. Y'all play too much."

Aunt Tina came out the patio door. "What happened up there? I could hear arguing, then it got quiet. I thought everything was good until I heard gunshots."

Tay tugged the hairs from his beard. "Gunshots? You heard gunshots?"

"Yeh. Gunshots. Did I stutter?"

"How many gunshots, Auntie?"

"I can't remember, maybe two or three."

"Hold on." He held up his index finger. "I didn't hear gunshots. I think you're hearing things. Did you drink some of this punch?"

Tina didn't look surprised. She and Casey gave each other a look.

"These must be some good drugs. Who wants to put in on more?" He joked.

Tina pursed her lips,

"Is everything a joke with you, Tay? Casey, get your son."

26
BRITTLE

July 5, 2020

Beep. Beep. Beep. Each pulse from his heartbeat alleviated her guilt momentarily. Brynn stood beside the hospital bed, holding Marc's hand, meditating on her decisions. *It should be me in this bed. He looks miserable and helpless. How did I let this happen?* She did what Brynn did best. Not stay in her lane. She wanted to fix him. Help him feel better. Heal him of his wounds. But she was confused. She didn't know what she wanted. She didn't know if she wanted him dead or alive. He could've used the mental health healing, but altering his mood wouldn't have erased the hole in his shoulder and stomach. We attempted to heal him. I reached out to touch his stomach since it seemed more life-threatening. Brynn turned to the door. She heard whispers. A doctor came in soon after and I shrank back. He stood at the foot of the bed.

"Surgery went well. He's a fighter." *He's a fighter, all right.* Brynn scoffed, thinking about him choking her. The doctor continued, "We were able to get the bullets out. What happened today?"

"Bullets? How many were there?"

"There were two bullets. One in his clavicle and one in his stomach." The doctor wanted to know, "How did this happen?"

Brynn got cheeky. "He got shot. You just said it."

"Yes, but how did this happen? Was there an altercation between him and someone else?"

"You mean, was this Black-on-Black violence?"

The doctor sighed. He got uncomfortable. "We need to know for our records."

"You need to know so you can call the police, but they were there. So, don't waste your time."

"This has already been reported. The police have come and gone. Marc wasn't awake, so nobody knows what happened."

"They know. Did the officer have two different colored eyes?" She wanted to know how much they knew.

"We're not at liberty to say. Is there anything else we need to be aware of?" They had some back-ass-wards rules if you ask me.

"No. I don't know. Like what?" Brynn was too angry to think about much.

"Prior illnesses, allergies, drugs?"

"Uh, yeh he does. Come on, Brynn, think." She couldn't hear me at all this time.

Brynn answered quickly, "I don't know. I can't remember. Didn't his mom come by?"

"Unfortunately, we haven't been able to reach family, and he didn't have a phone on him."

Brynn grabbed a nearby pen and notepad to write. She scrolled through her phone and wrote down a number. "Here." She tossed the paper onto his clipboard. The doctor watched as it slid down the page, hitting his stethoscope. "If you think of anything, just let the nurses know."

"Okay."

The doctor added, "Since you aren't related, we'll have to ask you to leave soon. I'm sorry."

The doctor left the door ajar, and as soon as the footsteps faded, I reached over and shut the door. Brynn thought to herself, *who is he to tell us to leave? He's not sorry. No one else is here. Marc needs me. I need to heal him, or else he won't survive.* After a few minutes of trying to heal him, nothing happened. Either her powers weren't working, or his wounds were worse than we thought.

I was still there, though. I was still alive, so it couldn't have been the powers. Maybe subconscious sabotage? Marc opened his eyes, shifting them in Brynn's direction. "How long have you been here?"

"Not too long. How are you feeling?" She put her hand over his.

He snatched it back. His upper lip flinched in disgust. "How do you think I feel?"

"I'm just trying to help you."

He turned away, looking out the window. "Yeh, you're good at that."

Brynn skulked. "Guess I'll leave then."

"Why did you do it?" Marc asked Brynn the same question GG had asked. He sounded like a hand puppet. I knew something was stuck up his ass.

Brynn acted oblivious, the same as she did before, "Why did I do what?"

"You know what you did."

"Marc, the doctor said your surgery went well." She tried to change the subject. She couldn't give him an answer, she didn't know why she did it. She didn't know why she tried to do one thing, and her hair did another. She had said numerous times before, "My hair does what it wants." Right? Right. So, I did. I made the tough decision to save him. It surprised me too. I knew if she let him die, she wouldn't have been able to live with herself. It was a foolish choice made in rash. She had intended to save him the whole time, but once I got closer, she decided it might be better if he sacrificed himself for her. Which was his plan anyway, evident by his standing up for her. I tried to shield him, but when she decided to push him at the last minute. It was a tug-o-war. Things got in disarray. He might have ended up dying, and just like I knew she would, she would have regretted it. Now that he's alive, she had to save him, but not for altruistic reasons this time. For shame.

Marc asked again, "Why did you push me?"

"I didn't push you," she looked up at the ceiling.

"Stop playing fucking games with me, bruh." He tried to reach for her arm but he drew back immediately, cringing from pain.

She stepped left out of his reach. "I was trying to push you out of the way."

"Well, good-fucking-job," he snarled.

She stopped by the next day with the goal of healing. There was a family outside praying. Brynn wished she could magically make their pain go away. She wished she could time travel and fix what was broken –bring back their loved one. Cure them. Heal them. Whatever they needed.

Brynn looked around the hospital, its shades of clinical, cold white coating every surface. She noticed the impartial look on the nurse's face, pretending they were fine when their cup runneth over with woe. But they had to pretend to keep going, as families broke down in front of them, leaving through the hospital doors with one less family member to love and be loved by. She hated the smell, it was a strong cocktail of bleach and disinfectant, it burned her nostrils and made her chest heavy because she knew they were trying to hide the smell of death. Marc had been put in a room that was usually meant for children and she felt exasperated by the decorations across the walls, children's imaginations put to paper to bring joy, knowing those same children were probably dying. All of it was too heavy. Worst of all were the gift shops she would pass every morning and every afternoon when she came and went, attending to Marc. She hated the gift shops. *Who's buying gifts? Who's buying this shit? I don't want to be here.*

She made multiple guilt-trips to the hospital. The compulsion to fix him was born from shame. Every day that he lay in that hospital was another layer of culpability. She sat in a chair waiting for Marc to wake up. A woman doctor stopped by.

"There's no easy way to tell you this. His diabetes is delaying the healing process. He's been here for two weeks, things look a little better, but we would have hoped for more by this point." Brynn shifted in her seat. Her eyes got big. She had forgotten about his diabetes. Which made me further lean toward subconscious sabotage. Maybe that was just my schtick. Brynn and I had also been trying to heal him for two weeks. Brynn was tired. I was tired. He wasn't healing. There was no hope. She thought that if she could get him home, she could work on him at night, too—round-the-clock care.

Brynn asked the doctor, "Is there something else we can try?"

"We've done all we can do." The doctor looked at the medical monitors.

"Have you, though?" Brynn got snarky because she was aware of the racial disparities experienced by Black people in hospital settings.

"Dear, I know how you feel. I'm sorry that this is happening, but only time will tell. We're going to keep him for as long as we can for observation." The doctor clasped her hands in front of her chest.

"What do you mean as long as you can?" Brynn raised an eyebrow.

"Oh," she said with an awkward pause. "He doesn't have insurance, so either way, we'll have to discharge him soon. Unless he has some family that can help?"

If I could have said two words to that doctor, they would have been generational poverty. Every time a white person mentions a Black person asking family for financial help, I get angry. We were slaves. Then we weren't paid fairly. We weren't hired. We were fired for stupid shit. We couldn't start a business. If we did, they would be burned to the ground. That's the tip of the iceberg. We broke. Brynn blinked at her in disgust.

"It's better to be in the comfort of home, anyway. My opinion." The doctor stuffed a hand in her white coat. Brynn sat forward, "You're talking like he's going to die. Is he going to die?"

"We're doing our best, but let's hope for full recovery sooner than later."

"Were you all able to get in touch with his mother? I gave that other doctor her phone number weeks ago."

"I'm afraid so. She said she would come by, but as far as I know, she never did. If you can get in touch with her, tell her it's best she does not wait."

Marc was discharged soon after. To prepare for his arrival, Brynn removed the pink sheets from her bed. She replaced them with the black ones that GG gave her when she first moved in. She bought new pillows. The firm ones, so he could sit up in bed instead of sinking. We all hate the sunken place.

She vacuumed and the rugs squealed from the sensation. The figures on the wall watched her and tidied up their spaces too, trying to reflect a sense of order and peace back to her. She disinfected the nightstand and the remote. She thoroughly cleaned the bathroom, top to bottom. All this to expunge the germs that might further inhibit healing... And all of this to expunge guilt. His acetaminophen, prescribed antibiotics, and a phone charger were waiting for him on the nightstand. Everything he needed for everything she had to give.

BEDHEAD

July 31, 2020

Brynn tugged at me from his side of the bed. I was being pulled down from his weight. I was raveled around his body—his right arm and leg, his stomach, his neck even. I could have choked him in his sleep. We worked nonstop. I was outstretched, overwhelmed, and overworked. We attempted to heal him day and night, even caring for him in our sleep. It had been a month since the BBQ. If I had to describe the tension in the apartment, I would have compared it to a downpour. I would compare it to the inland rainfall during a hurricane. It was loud. I couldn't focus. I couldn't hear myself think. I couldn't see past the storm we were standing in, as if it were hail. It was hell. I only remember it in flashes, so that's how I'll describe it. Yes, we were that worn out. Brynn had gone to the grocery store. Upon returning, she found Marc icing his wound. Marc had been complaining that his stomach had swelling. I think he gained weight from being immobile. A little jelly roll ain't never hurt nobody. Shit, I wanted to take a bite.

She barked at him, "What are you doing? The doctor said you need to keep it dry. The ice is going to melt, and it's going to get wet." Before he could respond, she already had me up against the wound to heal it in case of bacteria.

"Chill, I'm good." He pushed me away.

"Fine. I didn't want to do it anyway." I was getting bent out of shape again, and I had an attitude. Brynn repeated after me as if she could hear what I said.

"Fine. I didn't want –" Then she stopped herself, putting her hand over her mouth.

"You didn't want to what?" He asked.

"Nothing. I didn't want you to get an infection." She pursed her lips to the side.

"These sheets stank," he said sharply.

"I changed them before you got here. They were fresh out of the linen closet."

"They smell like mothballs." He tried to get out of the bed, but his foot slipped, and he slid onto the floor. I was thinking, since he's down there, leave his ass.

She got irritated with him. "You doing too much. Stay here. I'll change the sheets." Between the sheets, at night, that's when things got nasty. Bloody nasty. One night, Brynn awoke to Marc fidgeting with a medicine bottle, she sat up and waited for her eyes to adjust. "What are you taking?"

"Aspirin. I have a fever."

Brynn sighed. "Where did you find aspirin?"

"Under the bathroom sink. What's with the twenty questions?"

"The doctor said don't take aspirin because it can cause your blood to thin and cause bleeding."

I didn't mind that. I could've used a midnight snack.

Brynn goes on. "Anyway, how did you get to the bathroom alone? I thought you weren't feeling better."

Marc turned over and went back to sleep, snoring. She did the same. Not too long after, Marc shook her awake. "Brynn, Brynn. I'm bleeding." This wasn't the snack Brynn wanted, but it was the snack we needed—a boost in energy. Call me a vampire because his essence was my essence. His blood was my life force. Brynn hopped out of the bed and turned the light on. Rushing back to the bed, she applied pressure to his stomach wound with a nearby hand towel. Maybe, I wasn't getting that snack after all.

She stared at her phone. "If it doesn't stop bleeding in ten minutes, we have to call 911." She shook her head in disappointment. The time read 2:34 AM. She drew the corners of her mouth inward in an *I told you so* manner. Not wanting him to see her facial expressions or her look of disgust, she left the phone on the nightstand. So, that she would have to turn away from him to see it. At 2:40, she started to worry. "It's been six minutes." She laid her phone on the bed in front of her.

"Can't you use your hair?" He asked, despite his pride.

"You said you were good. You didn't want my help," she said with a petty tone.

"Why do you have to make me beg?"

"I didn't hear you ask, nor beg."

"I don't need this shit." He pushed her hand away again. "I'm going through enough without you hounding me."

"Hmph. The bleeding stopped." It took eight minutes. Brynn somehow knew without looking. Likely intuition because I had sopped it all up without her noticing. I felt refreshed. What truly rocked his grounds was how he felt mentally.

Marc started humming in his sleep one night. Brynn thought nothing of it initially, hoping it was a bad dream. The humming turned to a whine, so she poked him a bit. He didn't wake. Then it became a whine with intervals of hollering.

He shouted, "No! Stop! Please!" Hell, I didn't know please was in his vocabulary.

He was startled out of his sleep in a cold sweat. The next night, the same thing happened. Everything he knew so well became the biggest fear in his life. Everything was a trigger. Marc heard knocking. He jerked in his sleep, grunting at the noise. He heard the knocking again and popped up like a jack-in-the-box, shaking and checking the surroundings.

"Where am I?"

Knock-Knock! Brynn calmly rolled over. "It's fine. You're fine." She soothed him like a baby.

"Whose knocking at the door?" Marc reached for the drawer.

"Marc, you're fine. What are you reaching for?" Her tone got serious. "I know you ain't got a gun in that drawer?"

He pulled his hand back.

"Anyway," she moved out of bed. "It's the groceries I ordered yesterday."

"What? You're scared to leave me alone now? You think I'm a child?"

To me, the answer was obvious. "You may not be a child, but you're childish."

Brynn whispered, "childish," as she walked off, looking over her shoulder at him. I was curious. This was the second time she repeated something I'd said. She floated around with a slight burst of energy, even though I was disheveled and had bedhead. She put six pieces of bacon in a pan, cracked four eggs and put them into a bowl, poured in a tablespoon of milk, and sliced a pat of butter. Once the bacon was visibly crunchy, she scrambled the eggs and added a handful of shredded cheddar cheese. It was maximum cheesiness. The bread popped out of the toaster, she poured a glass of milk, and breakfast was made. I was flabbergasted. Breakfast in bed for the tyrant. Why?

"Here you go." She slid the plate and cup on the nightstand, shifting his things to the side.

He stared as she did it. "What am I, four? Why did you bring me a glass of milk?"

"You don't have to drink it."

He picked up the bacon, twisting it around. "I'm supposed to eat this dry-ass toast and this burnt-ass bacon with nothing to wash it down with?" He dropped it on the plate.

She took a deep breath, trying to be patient. "What do you want to drink then, Marc," she accentuated the C.

"You should be in this bed, not me," he growled. I snarled, because how dare he talk to Brynn that way?

"And you should be dead. Not Cory." She threw her hand up, quickly walking off, *finally* tired of his malarkey, but also afraid he might jump up and hit her.

"You're right. I should be. It's like death is gunning for me."

Did he really believe that? I wish I could have asked him because I knew this was haberdashery and games. A ploy to keep her quiet. I hoped that she wouldn't fall for whatever tomfoolery this was.

"I'm going to take a nap on the couch. I'm tired." Brynn motioned toward the den.

The boost of energy was short-lived. It could be compared to a thirty-minute nap after having unrelenting insomnia—a drop in the bucket. We slept, but when we were awake, we were either healing Marc, cooking, cleaning, or calming him down. The PTSD was no joke. After trying to fix him for weeks, I'm matted, dry, and still bent out of shape. I had never felt like that before. By this point, it had been about six weeks since our last perm. We needed a hair appointment. I felt like I was going to wither away. Speaking of which. *Oh shit, I missed my appointment, I need to call and reschedule soon.* Brynn lay on the couch facing the cushions with a leg propped up over the back. She started a new text to Almara.

I wished I could tell her what I saw the last time we were at the salon. "Brynn, I've been thinking and I don't think we should go to Almara anymore. She's a shapeshifter. She's hiding something. I felt it in my roots and I was right."

Brynn turned her head slightly to see behind herself as if she heard something, a whisper, she thought but continued to text. She might not have heard me, but I know she felt it in her bones.

"Hey, Almara! Do you have any availability soon? I needed a perm yester-week lol." She stared at the sent message, hoping for a quick reply, but that served only to help her doze off again. This girl says one thing and does another. She slept for two hours before being awakened by the sound of running water.

"Not again." She realized what was happening and hurried to the bathroom before Marc hurt himself further. It seemed like that's all he'd been trying to do.

"You could have woken me up," she said.

Naked, he inched into the bathtub one foot at a time, which had stretched itself wider like a mouth preparing to swallow. "I can bathe myself. I'm a grown-ass man." He was too egotistical to ask for help. Grown-ass men know how to ask for help.

She supported his body, holding onto his side as he entered the tub. "I don't think this is a good idea." She cautioned.

"There's barely any water in here. You trippin'. Pass me the washcloth." He held out his hand.

She watched as he washed his arms and face, surprised he could do that with the shoulder wound. Next, he washed half of his stomach, avoiding the wound. In an attempt to lean forward to wash his legs, he grimaced in pain, yeeting the washcloth forward into the wall.

Brynn flinched. "What the fuck?"

"This some bullshit, man. I'm a grown-ass man," he groaned, "and I can't even wash my own ass. This shit is fucked up, man."

He was miserable. It must've been awful to have been so vulnerable, naked, and wide open.

Brynn caught the rag before it sank into the water. "Lean up," she told him as she squeezed the wet rag, letting the warm water trickle down his back. "Let me help you."

She cleaned him of his wrongdoings, showering her love as unspoken forgiveness. She ran the rag around his leg, down to his feet, and back up the other leg. He rested, staring at himself in the faucet, seeing a distorted, false impression of a grown-ass man.

28
RINSE

August 16, 2020

"It's Sunday sinner check-in," Brynn's mom would say every time GG called. I wondered if she was talking about the people at the church or her mother. Every weekend it was a source of friction. GG would call mom every Saturday to see if she wanted to attend church the next day. Every Saturday, they would bicker. After the incident, Brynn lived with GG, and they went to church every Sunday.

"Remember, the church is for saints *and* sinners. All are welcome in the house of the Lord," GG wanted to cement the importance of Church into Brynn's head and offer a rebuttal for her daughter's conviction. Besides, we all know the rules when living under grown folks' roof. Their house, their rules. Nowadays, Brynn went to church every pink moon because she could only tell GG, "no," so many times before the guilt kicked in. Brynn didn't believe that the way to salvation was through the church. She wouldn't have considered herself a churchgoer, but this day, she decided to go to Church of her own volition. She needed a sign, a message, a word. She believed that if she decided to go to church that day at that moment that God would tell her exactly what she needed to do. She needed a message from the divine creator, but she didn't believe in the person delivering the message. Even if they claimed to be a man of God. That person is flesh, and flesh is weak, right? Not to be trusted.

Looking in the wall mirror of GG's living room, Brynn asked, "Do you have a hat that I can wear today?"

GG turned around to make sure she heard right. "You're not going to want to wear any of my hats."

"I need to cover this new growth. My hair looks terrible. I'm past due for a perm."

"That's not what they're for. Did you ever open that box I gave you?" GG trailed off, shaking her head in disappointment. She gave in. "They're in the room down the hall," she lazily gestured away from her body, not pointing in any specific direction.

Brynn opened the door, noticing that GG's collection had grown since the last time she was in there. Her hand rested on the doorknob as she scoped the room. There were green hats, black hats, silver hats, big hats, cup hats, some of them were moving around, swapping shelf space and trying to move closer to the scarves. The rhinestone hats sat high up on the top shelf by GG's necklaces, looking down on the other hats, making sure to avoid the gloves entirely. Brynn sneered. "Ew, rhinestone, that's tacky." The rhinestone hats vibrated in annoyance.

GG yelled from the other room. "You say something?"

"Nah, still looking."

GG mumbled under her breath, "I told you." Then she spoke louder, "hurry up if you're gonna get something. You know I don't like to be late and the hats don't like to be stared at, they like to be worn or left alone."

Brynn grabbed a classy black straw hat that had been slowly inching itself closer to her and she left.

'*Church*' is the structure you visit on Sunday. '*Chuch*' is the activity that goes on within the walls. It's over the top and operated by the spirit. One might think segregation still existed when visiting a Black church. It's a place for people to rebuild their souls after coming to blows with spiritual assaults on their lives. It's where people attempt to let go and cope with loss. It's where they pray to God to remove the obstacles in their way—usually placed there by themselves.

Churchgoers promise not to sin, fornicate, lie, or do another bad thing if God would help them. Walking through the door, an older woman dressed in all white with white gloves and white shoes reached her hand out toward Brynn and GG. The ushers were always so supportive and welcoming. Whatever you need, they got you –a seat, a few tissues, a hug, anything. GG put her hand inside the woman's hands and said, "Good Morning, sister." GG seemed so different at church. The woman's white gloves tickled GG's hands with delight. Brynn nodded and kept moving.

We sat in the front, in GG's favorite seat. The co-pastor and backbone of the church, the first lady, sat not too far away. Sometimes she was allowed to preach but only when the pastor was away, being a visiting preacher for another church. Her spirit was that of a civil rights activist. She wanted to make a change. Brynn sat with her shoulders back and her hands in her lap, one hand cupping the other. As the preacher entered, Brynn watched his every move –every step, gesture, and facial expression. She attended to the words coming out of his mouth and the sweat beading his forehead. She wondered if he had been rushing to get here. Was he hot? Was he about to tell a lie? Why was he sweating? Someone brushed her back to get to their seat. She leaned forward slightly but kept her attention on the pastor. Nothing would break her concentration. She didn't want to miss the message. We had a one-eyed preacher. He didn't walk around with a patch on his eye, but he could only see out of one eye. The good eye was brown. The bad eye was brown swirled with grey. He said it was cataracts, but no one believed him because he never talked about getting surgery, the easiest solution. Most church rumors were that he had some age-related degeneration or unmanaged diabetes. He admitted to neither. Standing at the pulpit like he had a lot on his mind, the preacher opened his Bible, "I'm not going to take up too much of y'all time this morning. I want to get directly into the word of God." That was the first lie. He continued. "Today is truly the day that the Lord has made. I got a word for y'all." Brynn fixed her posture to hear better. Pausing to look down, the preacher goes on. "It's my prayer that

God would speak to you in the midst of these hard times. It is my hope that he would shine a light on your life in some divine way and that he would answer a question that you have laid before him. That he would minister to you. Stand on your feet. Let us pray." The church stood. Books, purses, feet, and hungry stomachs shuffled as they moved. The preacher prayed. "Father, I invite you into this house. I pray, God, that by your glory, you would use me to be a blessing to somebody. I pray that you will show your sufficiency in the lives of every person here. In the name of Jesus, we pray. Let the church say Amen."

"Amen," they echoed.

"While you're standing, hug the person next to you, and tell them, 'You are more than enough.'" Brynn liked the hugs. I found this process repulsive. It's a case of who can collect the most germs. Everybody shuffled back to their seat and the piano started.

"You may be seated." The sound of weight bumping the pews was simultaneous. A handful of ladies remained standing. Those are the ones that will catch the holy ghost later.

"Turn with me, in your Bibles, to St. John chapter six, verses one to nine," the preacher instructed. "I'll give you time to get there." He cleared his throat so he could speak with exaggerated preacher inflection. "Everybody who's pulling on you takes from you. Come on now. Talk to me, somebody. No matter how much you love 'em. I'm talking about your boo, your baby, TeeTee, cousin Black, your mama, your grandma, all of them. Can we be honest with y'all this morning? They can be draining."

The preacher read John chapter six, verses one to nine, but I'll sum it up Brair-style: Jesus had just healed a man. So, a gang of people was like *lehgo*! Let's follow Jesus! So, they did. It was Passover, and Jesus sat with the disciples. He asked Phillip where they could get enough bread to feed the followers, about 5,000, to be exact. He was testing Phillip. Phillip said, we got a lil' bit of bread, but it ain't finna be enough. One of the disciples, Andrew, said there's a boy here with five barley loaves and two fish, but that won't be enough either. Everybody split the crumbs, and Jesus, with his magical grace, ensured they were full.

The preacher went on, "You are more than enough." He said, "look at your neighbor, and say Amen." The cymbals flared. GG looked at Brynn and said, "Amen." Brynn looked at GG and nodded. I never noticed how demanding the preacher was until now. Say amen, hug your neighbor, stand up, say this, do this with your hands, look here, pay this, don't do this, sit boo-boo sit. He preached with the vigor of a man accused of murder, trying to prove his innocence. He stomped his feet between sentences, frolicking around the stage. One could've mistaken it with displeasure if they didn't know better. If they were the *type* to mistake passion for anger. The preacher continued his sermon: "God said, I meant for you to be overwhelmed. You are a limited resource. No matter how you love people, you can't be there for everybody. I want you to forgive yourself for not having enough because the weight and the pressure is on every last one of us to be more than enough. The truth of the matter is, that you don't have enough. You have the passion, but you don't have enough product. You have the love, but you don't have the resources. This is a setup. You need to discover the Lord. Say no. You can't be everywhere...God wants to use you in a mighty way, and God has a plan for your destiny. I'm tired. I'm just being honest. I'm tired of people. I can't help everybody else until I'm okay. ...God said you're not enough. I'm going to make you more than enough. I will do a miracle in your life that you will not run out. You don't have to be tired, exhausted, bitter, and snapping at people. I am going to strengthen what you already have...You're lost. Release the burden. Release the guilt. Release the shame. That's why I gave you the gift. To help yourself."

The organs timbre with bass. GG threw her hand in the air, praising God on what seemed like a calculated time interval. "Hallelujah," she hollered. I wondered if she was listening. The message couldn't have been clearer. Brynn knew what God wanted, and she knew what she needed. She kept playing back the words in her head. *I'm more than enough. I'm tired. My power is for me.*

GG clapped to the music, bobbing her head in unison. A woman shook her hand tambourine, distracting Brynn from the sermon. She noticed a kid eating cookies at the end of the pew, and it reminded her of Cory and his mom's cookies. She could've used a cookie at that moment. Some conversation too. She whispered to GG, "Do you want to get something to eat after?" She made sure to ask before GG started talking to everyone for an hour after service. For someone who didn't talk much, GG sure seemed to have a lot to say on Sundays. GG stopped clapping to glimpse at Brynn, then nodded in agreement as Brynn had done earlier. It felt playfully petty, but nothing served to be as petty as the confrontation that was about to take place at brunch.

29
THE CHAIR SPIN

"Yep, they called me a mutt." Thinking back, she snickered. Almara stood before a small group of new stylists inside her hair salon. They sat on folding chairs in the middle of the room. This day, Almara preferred to be in her base form because of the implications captured within. She needed to gain the trust of her recruits. Most of them, mixed like herself, had been called mutts before too.

"It's cool, though. I've had plenty of time to deal with the loss of my parents. I know what I am and it's not a mutt. I'm a product of love and unity. Same as y'all. That's my goal for us. Equality."

The group made eye contact with each other, questioning the validity of her motivation. They looked to Mary for corroboration. Mary, a dyed-in-the-wool bigot, leaned against a nearby doorway in her navy pleated pants, light blue blouse, and tan loafers. She could've cared less about how or why they did it, but anything to keep Brown down. She was the plug, that's where Almara got her product. Mary liked to sit in on training sessions to ensure her investment remained fruitful. She walked over, and stood next to Almara, nodding in agreement. "It's like neutering a dog. You want to keep that aggressive behavior at bay. That's why we're here, right?" she said condescendingly. "It's for their benefit in the long run."

"I want us to be equal. I want fairness," Almara repeated, taking a step from Mary.

"Yeh, that," Mary mumbled under her breath, looking away.

Almara blinked rapidly, continuing the discussion. "Now that I've told you about my background and why I came to America, do you all have any questions?"

A young woman raised her hand. She pulled her curly marmalade hair behind her ear. "Why didn't you shift for the pencil test?"

"If I had shifted to white, as I assume you mean, then I would have had to leave the only family I knew. There would have been no time to say goodbye. I'd hoped for the best but hadn't expected the worse. Besides, that white woman never left my sight. I could only imagine what they would have done to me for being a witch instead—maybe hung, maybe set on fire, maybe both? Not a fate I wanted to test."

The woman went on like a teacher's pet. "Why didn't you shift for the job interview?"

"I thought America was better than home. I was naïve."

"How did you learn about relaxers? That they did what they do? You know, that they were dampeners?" The young woman bit her lip and raised her eyebrows.

Almara snapped her fingers and smoothed into pointing at her. "What's your name?"

"Christine," the young woman answered in a low voice.

"First of all, Christine, get in the habit of calling it a relaxer. And with the quickness. Secondly, I tried a relaxer for the first time when it got popular in the 80s. After the relaxer was in, I noticed that I couldn't fully shift. I could lose the skin color, but not the curls." She fluffed her hair. "I could change my eye color, but the freckles remained. I thought it had something to do with the new environment. I thought, maybe stress related. After a day or two, I got caught in the rain. We all know how that goes. At that moment, I could shift effortlessly. That's when I realized."

"How did you find the girl, your subject?" Christine pulled out a mini notebook and clicked her pen.

"The same way some of you found yours. Windfall. But with that being said, let's shift the topic. I want to know why you're all here today. And since you're already standing and clearly like to talk, you go first." Almara made eye contact with Christine, standing with her hands on her hips.

Christine clasped her arms behind her body. She fiddled with the pen and paper. "Well, I want to help them. I don't want them to end up in jail, hurt, or dead. I don't think they know what they're doing. They are letting their hair control them."

"That's no excuse," a brunette with long, loose curls shouted out of turn.

"You wouldn't blame a mentally ill person for their actions. Would you?" Christine asked.

"No, you're right. I'd have thrown their ass in the crazy house," the brunette cackled, along with some of the other recruits.

Christine brought her arms back around, crossing them as she swirled her neck. "You're delusional."

"No. I think it's you that's delusional. You belong in the crazy house with them bat-shit crazy bitches if you think they need help." The brunette dapped a woman next to her as they laughed louder.

Another recruit stood up. She had thin lips, and her skin had a tinge of orange like she ate carrots daily for lunch. "There's one at my job. An outsider."

"What did she do?" The brunette stood up and asked.

"I haven't seen her do anything yet, but I know she has powers."

"Then how do you know? Did she tell you?"

The orange lady placed her hands in her olive plaid blazer pockets. "I just know. I can feel it. She walks around the office like she's better than us, with her resting bitch face and long fingernails. She has her own office too. There's no way she got that job on her own. She had to have done something to get ahead.

Affirmative action can only get you so far." She narrowed her eyes looking out the window behind Almara.

A man in a wheelchair yelled from the back. "One of them took a dangerous situation into their own hands. It cost me my leg."

"How are you going to do hair in a wheelchair?" The brunette was bullying folks at this point.

The man responded, "Ever heard of a prosthetic leg, dumb ass."

A girl in purple cowboy boots popped out of her seat. She blurted, "One of them killed my dog." Then, she popped back into her chair. The group snickered. Almara placed her hand in the air as if to say stop. They were getting out of pocket.

"Have a seat. Everybody, have a seat." She waved her hand up and down.

Christine poked her butt back into the seat. The brunette plopped into hers. The orange lady slowly slid into hers.

"I said it before, and I'll say it again, we need to be unified. Y'all are not giving me good vibes. Moving on. Any other questions about the process?"

Christine stood back up with her notebook, not giving anyone else a chance to speak. "What age do we start relaxing?"

"Most of them start getting relaxers at a very early age. That's why this method has been successful. We start young before the powers have surfaced."

Christine asked, "What do we tell them? I would feel bad lying to them."

Almara's nostrils flared as she scratched her nose. "We don't lie. They usually assume the powers come from the perm. Your job is to make sure their hair is laid. Can you do that?"

August 16, 2020

T he vibe was burgundy. Brynn and GG made their way to Downtown East Point for brunch. The area was booming with Black people, but the buildings gave off a slavery vibe. They were made out of red clay brick and had the same bones and foundation from the late 1800s. Put it this way, many of the houses still had pillars, and a lot of plantation-style houses have pillars. I'm not saying that one begets the other, but I am saying that the other begets the one. Cash Only Diner was brick inside and out. Inside, the bricks were a combination of plum red and brown bricks. As soon as you entered, there was bar-style seating smack dab in the middle. The stools were bright red with silver bottoms, as one would expect from a diner. The booths were red leather with channel tufting. The roof venting and electrical were exposed—all these combined to give it a hole-in-the-wall, industrial aesthetic. Old 80s music played overhead on a loop. In the middle, the kitchen sat behind the U-shaped bar seating. One could hear every pot clang and every dish crash. Every order yelled, and every order-up bell. Seated at a booth, GG shuffled through her purse for her readers. Brynn sat quietly, picking at the skin around her fingernails. GG finally put on her readers, scanning the menu as if she were going to get something different today. She's picky, and this was her favorite place to eat. She already knew what she wanted. Brynn followed suit and picked up the menu. As reluctant as she was to ask for help, she knew it was what she needed. Even seeming like a know-it-all, GG did know a lot.

"GG, I need some advice. I didn't tell you, but I went to the doctor a few months back, and the doctor said that I should stop getting perms because... It's bad for my health."

GG gently placed her menu on the table, "Go on."

"What do you mean 'go on?' I just told you something was wrong with me."

"You said you needed advice. What's the question?"

Brynn's eyes squinted. "Should I stop perming?" She asked. "I won't have my abilities anymore. My stylist never responded about setting an appointment anyway. It's been like two weeks. Plus, I got a bad feeling about her anyway."

"You –"

Before GG could get a sentence out, the server came by.

"Good morning, I'm Sharon. You ladies know what you want, or do you need a minute?"

GG looked over the top of her readers. "I'll have a cup of freshly made black coffee, and the fried catfish and grits. Over-easy eggs with toast."

Brynn thought back to the cookies. "I'll have milk. Add ice, please. To eat, I'll get the chicken and waffles. Thanks."

Sharon stuffed her tiny notepad back into her apron. "Got it."

GG was about to speak but Brynn's phone vibrated. "I'll be right back. Going to the ladies' room," GG muttered.

Ding! The bell rang. Someone yelled from the kitchen, "Order up!"

Brynn picked up her phone. It was Marc wanting to know when she would be back. After staring at the text for a while, she put the phone down with the screen still on and stared more. She tried to reply to Marc several times, deleting what she had written over and over, trying to stay strong, but she wanted to curse him out. Finally, she put the phone face down.

An austere voice approached from behind, "I said I don't know. I haven't seen her." Brynn slightly turned around to look out of the corner of her eye, seeing a woman hang up the phone without saying bye. She was a redhead with loose and fluffy curls.

The woman kept talking as she bumped against the seat behind Brynn. "Sorry about that, Zoe. I don't know why he keeps calling me. Where was I?"

I recognized that voice. "It's her," I said to Brynn. "It's that double-crossing shapeshifting bitch." Brynn turned her head faintly as if trying to hear a voice in the wind. She could feel my tetchiness in her bones. She could feel my veracity vibrate her soul. Zoe sat down across the table. She had curly blonde hair and blue eyes, but not in the typical sense. There was a hint of brown in her skin. Like a little coffee with her milk. "You were telling me about the girl that came to you after she..." Zoe leaned forward and whispered, "killed her mother."

Brynn still had her head turned.

"Oh yeh. Okay, so her grandmother brought her to me only a few days after that happened." The woman continued.

"I want to know how she did it," Zoe asked with wide eyes, still leaning forward on the table.

"I don't know how, but she did say the girl killed her mother with her own hair. That's why she was bringing her to me. So that I could get that in check." She held up a finger, "Do you remember those parkgoers back in May? How they described the girl that was whacking people around at Southern Peaks with her hair? That's her. That's the one."

I couldn't believe it. "Brynn, she's talking about you. Did you hear what she said?" I felt Brynn's body temperature increase.

Ding! "Order up!"

Zoe frowned, "Damn. She's crazy. Can you imagine killing your own mother? The person that gave you your life and you take it from them. That's some evil, grimy shit." She looked down at her menu but quickly looked back up. "You know what, I get it now. There's too much violence in this world as is. They need to be put on a leash." She paused, pushing the menu back to the table. "But one more question, why you? Why did the grandmother come to you?"

"I knew her. Rather, I know her. We *were* friends. We met after I moved to Atlanta. We went on a double date way back in the day, and she almost killed her date with her powers. I tried to help her too. Tried to relax her. Especially after I found out she was pregnant by him. But she wouldn't let me. I had made the mistake of telling her that I couldn't shift when I first tried one. But I always kept in touch because, well, the apple doesn't fall too far from the tree if you know what I mean. She ended up having four daughters, including the one that the girl killed."

"Hold on wait… so, she's been putting shit in your head, in me, and that shit weakens us! So, does that mean if you go natural, then I'm here to stay? Oh, Brynn, imagine what we could do without being stifled."

Zoe nodded, "I get you, because they're clearly a family of psychos."

The woman motioned at her surroundings, "Heck, she and I used to eat here for breakfast sometimes. Well, at their old location in Decatur back in the day."

Brynn was hot. She now knew what the perms did, but the *real* truth hadn't hit her yet.

GG slid back into her seat, noticing Brynn distracted, ear-hustling. She knew Brynn wanted advice but I knew how GG thought. She wasn't about to repeat everything she'd told Brynn that morning after jail. Nothing had changed in her eyes, so why waste her breath?

The redhead fanned herself and a scent hit Brynn. "Grandma, are you wearing that perfume?"

GG sat with her hands crossed in her lap. "What perfume, dear? I have so many."

Brynn became nippy. "That one with the vintage bottle. You know the one. It had a burgundy top. It smelled all fruity and floral and crap."

I kept telling her what she already knew. "Brynn, you already know it's her. You smelled it at the hair salon. It's unmistakable."

Brynn shifted in her seat to look behind her. She peered at the woman's hair, studying every strand and coil. It reminded her of the woman from the protest.

But the woman from the protest was white. This one had fair skin, and her freckles were aplenty. She gave the woman a swift squint and suddenly, she knew. She knew the truth. She knew what I'd been trying to tell her since the end of June. Suddenly that gut feeling came through. Brynn scooted out of the booth and leaned against the end of the woman's table with one arm. Zoe's eyes got big. Zoe looked down at Brynn's hand, then looked at the redhead. The redhead flinched an eyebrow and gave Brynn a phony smile.

Brynn ignored Zoe, directing her attention to the redhead. "Speak of the devil, and she shall appear. Like you, the devil takes many forms, huh Almara?"

Almara's nose did that thing, "Do I know you?"

"Really? Give me a break. I didn't take you as a gutless wench. Your hair looks just like the day of the protest. Same curl pattern. Same length. Except for the color, of course. You sound like her too. Like you drink pumpkin spice lattes for lunch. You even got that stupid wrinkled nose. But it was that damn perfume that gave you away. I heard what you said about me."

Ding! "Order up!"

Beef for breakfast, anyone? There was about to be beef. Speaking of which, I hadn't eaten in quite a while. I was bloodthirsty. Almara stood up next to Brynn and pulled at the bottom of her shirt, "And? Can I help you?"

GG glared at Almara as she stood. Now knowing why Brynn was asking, GG rolled her eyes from Almara to Brynn, finally answering Brynn's question, "Oh, you mean my Design perfume?" She cleared her throat for a phony greeting, "Alma."

Almara replied, "G."

"See, Brynn, I told you. Up to no good. That heifer said you were a bad apple. And not only do she and GG know each other, but they're on a nickname basis and shit. What is that?"

Brynn was too flabbergasted to move. Brynn looked at GG sideways with scrunched eyebrows and her mouth slightly open. She finally spoke, as she stood straight at a snail's pace. "Alma, huh? Okay, so it's true," Brynn said with a tone of betrayal.

Almara's crinkled her nose again. "Damn G, you hadn't told her yet?"

GG deflected, "You never could trust those shapeshifting bitches." It was as if she was speaking from experience.

"But you know her." Brynn almost forgot who she was talking to, GG gave her that watch-your-mouth look. Brynn scratched her forehead with one finger. She looked back at Almara. "Why are you here? And why are you disguising yourself? Are you Black? Are you white? Are you light-skinned or dark-skinned? What's the goal?"

Almara laughed, looking at the roots of me, "I see you got some new growth." At that moment, I could see why GG and Almara were friends. Can anybody answer a question around here?

Ding! "Order up!"

Brynn's head titled. Almara's words played back in her head, *I had made the mistake of telling her that I couldn't shift when I first tried one.* Brynn took a deep breath, irately biting her bottom lip. "I could've saved his life, couldn't I? I could have saved Cory if you weren't putting that shit in my hair. I wouldn't have been too tired, too weak to save him." Brynn's thoughts were racing, connecting all the dots. "You're out here playing games with people's lives and it's costing others theirs."

GG crossed her arms and shook her head, leaning back on the red leather.

"Almara smirked, feeling dignified. "It's for the greater good. You don't need that power. You would abuse it. Well, you already have."

"Your wanna-be-white-today-Black-tomorrow ass doesn't know shit about what I would do. You're just the help."

"You ain't got to be white to be right."

"You ain't got to steal land to catch these hands," Brynn lunged at Almara, wrapping her hands around Almara's throat. Almara grabbed Brynn by her shirt and rammed her into the side of the booth. GG just sat there, with a front-row seat, watching as if it were an MMA fight, Roots x Roots. I couldn't understand why she just sat there, but there was no time to try and find out. I grew. I grew across the room, sectioning myself into a myriad of thick appendages, waving through the air with heinous implications. It reminded me of that day in 6th grade. We didn't care if people were looking. They whispered. They gasped. They were stock-still as they watched from afar. It was mysterious, mesmerizing. Their mouths flung open. Almara made eye contact with Zoe as if begging for help. But she knew better. She knew what it was.

"Two-timing, double-crossing BASTARD!" We looked like a feral beast –a walking lick. Cthulu in this bitch.

"Get off me, you unkempt bitch." Almara was pissed off. It was like Brynn had said a trigger word and activated a sleeper agent. She reached for me. Grabbing hair, what a cheap way to win a fight. I slapped her hand down and I too wrapped around Almara's throat, slowly lifting her in the air, she hovered off the ground. That's when Almara's skin turned white. Freckles disappeared from her face. Her eyes turned green, then brown again. The freckles reappeared. Her features were switching, blinking like Christmas lights. Like that day at the salon.

GG stood up franticly, "Stop. Stop now," she yelled with a cracked voice and a tired tone. "You can't keep doing this." GG pulled me back. One piece after the other, she pulled the tresses of me from around Almara's supple neck. Brynn looked at GG with a crossed face. She wondered what GG meant. *Can't keep doing what?*

Almara's feet rested on the floor. She took two steps back. "You proved my point. Look at you," Almara said to Brynn. "You're exactly the person you claim not to be."

Tired, Brynn plonked down in the booth, not a scratch on her face. "Whatever. You deserve it."

Almara snatched her belongings and walked out of the restaurant, not acknowledging Zoe. Nor had Zoe acknowledged her.

GG did what she did best. The tips of her hair wiggled. The onlookers mumbled, "What's going on?" They looked at each other, many confused, scared. I could hear someone from the kitchen, "The bacon is burning, what are you doing?"

Brynn was too mad for tears. She stared at her glass of milk. It reminded her of better days. Days when someone would listen and someone would talk. Days when she had a more compassionate shoulder to cry on. Days with Cory.

GG calmly sat down, not yet uttering a word. Brynn was still replaying everything that went on.

After minutes of silence, their food arrived.

GG nodded, speaking to Sharon, "Suga, can I get some hot sauce?"

"Yes, ma'am." Sharon looked at Brynn. "Do you need anything?"

Brynn didn't even look up. Sharon could sense the tension, and took that as a cue to leave.

GG glanced at Brynn before taking a bite. "You got some egg on your face."

"I didn't order eggs, GG."

"I know."

31
TONE

August 16, 2020

G G played with her food, moving it around on the plate. She never finished a meal. Brynn couldn't bear to look her in the eyes. How dare she, after how she'd acted? GG didn't raise Brynn to act like a fool. She didn't raise her to let her emotions get the better of her: "You can catch more flies with honey than with vinegar," I could hear her voice in Brynn's head. Even when Brynn took a peek up, GG wasn't looking at her either. You could slice the tension with a sword.

"What did she mean I killed my mom?"

"Don't let her manipulate you, honey."

Brynn knew GG was bullshitting. "Stop, please. Just be honest, Grandma."

GG put her fork down, finally looking at Brynn. "You didn't mean to do it."

"So, you knew this whole time? About everything?"

"I carry burdens that others aren't equipped to carry."

"No, you needed to control the situation," Brynn regurgitated GG's same words from the BBQ. She was treading a thin line between disrespect and having had enough. "Why did you take me to her?"

"You wanted a perm, and you'd been asking for some time. That day, you came home from school and busted through the door hysterically, in tears. I was sitting on the couch. There was blood on your pink shirt. Your hair was all over the place like you'd been in a fight or something. You said some kid had been picking on you and they cut your hair in class because they couldn't see the

182

board...Your hair was in the way, you said. Your mother came out of the kitchen to see what was wrong. She was drying her hands on a dish towel, and then you blurted out that you wanted a perm. I was sitting on the couch across the room, you just kept going on and on about the perm. This had been something you'd asked for over and over. She said no, again, and kept asking you about the blood on your shirt. You were so mad. You weren't yourself anymore. You asked again, and she started to panic, trying to find out what had happened, first yelling over your screaming and crying, then pleading, trying to calm you down. It was back and forth until it wasn't and at that moment, I chose not to intervene. She must've known about your powers because she was adamant that you stay natural."

"This can't be right. This doesn't sound like me," Brynn shook her head.

"Well, I remember it like it was yesterday. Your hair must've grown forty feet before it flew across the room like a viper, striking your mother in the chest. The hit knocked her into the wall and onto the floor. I jumped up off the couch but before I could get to her, you suddenly realized what you'd done. You were still standing at the front door, but you wanted to help her up. The look of panic on your face was of genuine guilt, you looked between me and her with so much fear, so much shock, you didn't move. You tried to use your hair to get her to her feet, but you were so young and the powers were so new that when you tried to help her, you helped a little too much. Her feet weren't touching the ground anymore. You squeezed her so tight. Too tight. You didn't let go. You couldn't let go. My poor baby, oh my poor Felice. You just squeezed her until..." GG lifted her head up toward the ceiling. "Oh Lord, rest in power, my love. God bless her soul."

"I'm so sorry, Grandma. I never meant—"

"I didn't have the luxury of mourning at that moment. You were a child, and I had to clean up your mess, so I let you have what you wanted, a perm. As you know your father left that day, so it was just me left to make any decisions. I didn't have the strength to fight with a little girl. That, combined with the school incident, having a lid on wouldn't hurt. Your temper was out of control. I'd never seen anything like it before. I had to allow you to learn the trouble that came with perms on your own."

"So, you let that woman hurt me? You could have guided me, taught me, explained my powers to me!" Brynn felt betrayed.

"Watch your tone."

"There's nothing wrong with my tone. It's the words you don't like. The truth."

"I've done everything for you. I've bent over backward for you. I helped you forget so you wouldn't be burdened by the pain of your powers. I wanted you to be happy, have some normality. Don't be ungrateful."

"Do I look happy? I smile. I laugh. I'm strong. I'm intelligent, but I'm not happy. This whole time, I thought I would die trying to help everyone else. Sacrificing myself for nothing."

"You had to learn that lesson on your own, even if it took a decade. You can lead a horse to water, but you can't make it drink. Your mother had good intentions, she wanted the best for you, and she loved you unconditionally. She was trying to protect you and keep you strong. Her experiences in life, the inequities she faced, that's what she paid. She passed down her equity to you that day."

"Wait. Hold on. What do you mean helped me forget?"

GG shifted in her seat, seeming restless. "Yeah," she responded matter-of-factly. She handed Brynn a $50 bill. "Take this and go pay. We'll talk in the car."

Brynn was barely in the car before she could ask, "You have powers too?"

"Where do you think you got them?"

"You never talk about it. We never talk about it."

"It's not something any of us talk much about. Do you think we would be safe if people knew? Not just rumors, but knew for real. They kill us for being black. Could you imagine? Black and a so-called witch. Besides, the perm usually dampens powers way more than they did for you. I had no idea *you knew* you had powers until the day at Southern Peaks. And by the way, that's the kind of stuff that gets us killed."

"I mean, not talking about these things will also get us killed too. How do you know what I did?"

"Your Aunt Casey saw you."

"What the f—" Brynn stopped herself.

GG could recognize that tone a mile away. "Watch your mouth. You showed out enough for one day."

"And I feel better for it. What do you mean she saw? Aunt Casey wasn't there. This isn't making any sense." Brynn paused. "Wait, she has powers too? All of us have powers, that's what Almara said, All four of your daughters had powers. What's hers?"

"Your Aunt Casey can see things as they're happening. Think clairvoyant, but only in the present."

"And you?"

"I don't know what to call it. I take memories, and I eat them. Technically, I drink memories."

Brynn looked at GG from the passenger seat, "Wow! My grandmother is a thief. That's a sin, you know." She was feeling better, and masking her emotions, so she wanted to lighten the mood.

"Child, you are pushing it today, and I don't steal. I borrow."

"Okay. You ever give them back?" Brynn tested.

"Accidentally, once. I gave a man a memory that didn't belong to him. He's dead now."

It seemed like Almara was right about that too. "How many memories of mine have you stolen? I want them back."

"I can't do that," she turned her head to the right, toward Brynn, but she was still looking at the road. Avoidance runs in the family.

"The word, *can't,* shouldn't be part of your vocabulary," Brynn repeated a phrase that GG had told her time and time before. "You can. My memories belong to me, so they shouldn't kill me."

"If only you knew." GG sighed.

"I will know once you give them back. What's my mom's...." Brynn hesitated, missing her mom, feeling guilt, "...I mean, what were her powers?"

"She could produce an antioxidant behavior within a person's body, healing almost any sickness, illness, or ailment."

Brynn thought. *That'd be nice to have with these damn fibroids. But I guess I could stop perming. That would help too.*

When they got to GG's house, Brynn hadn't even taken a seat before she started back up.

"So, how about those memories now?" She was serious about getting them back. She planned to convince GG and, if that failed, coerce her with guilt and gin.

"I wouldn't even begin to know what to do."

"Well... How do you steal... I mean, borrow the memories in the first place?"

"My hair does this thing, and then the memories go into the berries in my cane. I make a concoction with the berries, the memories and herbs. Then drink it."

"So, you don't know. I hope you wrote this down somewhere for your future great-great-grandchild that gets the same powers as you."

"Word of mouth."

"How? When nobody talks about anything. Boomers, I tell you," Brynn giggled.

GG smiled out of sight of Brynn.

"I'm just guessing here, but maybe you do the thing with your hair and will your intentions. Your hair thieves will instinctively know to regurgitate the memory, and I'll have it," Brynn shrugged.

GG pulled a bottle from her closet that read, 'Death's Door Gin,' "Go get two shot glasses from the cupboard."

It seemed as if Brynn wouldn't have to do much coercing.

"Why is there gin in your closet? Never mind, I'll stay in my lane but, drinking... In the afternoon... Together?"

GG asked, "Sober pain or drunk pain? Which do you prefer?"

Brynn scurried to the kitchen, returning with two shot glasses and the salt shaker. After all the drama, it felt good to have a moment like this with GG, it felt like a break. GG sat at the end of her bed while Brynn sat in a wicker chair across from her. "How long have you had this chair? I'm surprised it hasn't fallen apart."

"Magic." Their shot glasses cling-clang, toasting their first shot.

"The chair too?" Sometimes, Brynn could be ditsy.

"Nah, girl, that's a regular ole' chair. The chair in the living room though, make sure to sit on that one nicely. She's temperamental." GG laughed, grabbing the bottle for a second shot.

"Already?"

GG poured the shots. "Don't pretend like you can't keep up. You're my blood." Together, they threw two more shots to the back of their throat.

"Okay," Brynn stood from the chair. "I'm ready to see what happened. Hit me."

GG held up an index finger and said, "I was thinking."

"GG, don't do this."

"Did you open that gift I gave you?"

Brynn lay on GG's bed and lied, "Yes."

GG turned around and put her hand on Brynn's. GG's hair fluttered, and Brynn started to tremble. Her eyes rolled to the back of her head, only the whites were visible. GG squeezed Brynn's hand tighter. "Dear God, bring her through," she prayed. The trembles stopped, and Brynn's eyes closed. She didn't move. GG reached toward Brynn's neck for a pulse, but Brynn popped up before she could touch her. Rubbing her forehead, Brynn whispered, "You gave me too many."

"Too many shots? You're drunk?"

Brynn's eyes widened, staring at the blank wall in front of her. "No. You gave me some of your memories."

At her age, I was shocked GG hadn't mastered this, but then again, she did like to keep things to herself.

"What did you see?"

Beating around the bush, Brynn said, "there used to be a picture here." She pointed at the wall. As the memories started to come together, she stood. "I'm going home."

"I'm not letting you leave my house drunk. You can lay here and take a nap."

Brynn rolled her eyes and snickered. "GG, I don't get drunk from a few shots." She got her purse. She was uncharacteristically calm. *I don't want to be here. I can't be here.*

The door shut behind Brynn and GG picked up the phone, "Casey, I think I messed up."

"Hey Ma, are you okay? What happened?"

"I tried to give baby-girl her memories back."

"Oh Lord, mamma. Where is she now?"

"Getting in her car, in my driveway."

"Okay, I'll check on her in about thirty minutes to see what she's up to."

GG added, "And again an hour after that. She said I gave her some of my memories and then she left like nothing happened. Reminded me of myself at her age."

"Yeh, and we know that's not good."

"Hush, child."

"You spoil these grandkids. If that had been me back in the day, you would have snatched my ass back in the door. Anyway, it's gon' to be aight, Mama. I'll call you back when I know something."

32
SHEARS

August 16, 2020

"Where is that gift box?" Brynn shuffled through the things on the kitchen counter, moving old mail. She snatched the junk drawer open and it screamed from her shoving things around, having its insides re-arranged like that. "Where is that shit?" There it was, somehow all the way in the back. She untied the pink bow and delicately pulled off the top.

"Scissors?!" She said, bemused.

Holding the box in her hand, the image of a gold bracelet flashed in her mind. A gift from her mother on her twelfth birthday, only days before *the incident*. Brynn wondered where it was. She wanted to hold it again, wear it. She wanted to hold her mom again. She longed to hug her, to be hugged by her. She felt embarrassed for what she had done, embarrassed for how she acted in the liquor store the day she saw her dad, how ignorant she must have seemed to him, how cruel. Her head shook as if the memories would fly out. Then a memory that wasn't hers came about. An unconscious man, naked on a bed. GG, Almara, and another man stood around him. Was he dead? Did they kill him?

"What am I supposed to do with fucking scissors?" She hadn't decided if she would cut someone or something, but she would use those scissors. Brynn was bombarded with glimpses from that day in 6th grade. His words replayed in her mind, *tomorrow, I'll bring my scissors.* That fucker threatened to cut her hair. He threatened to cut me, I remembered it now too. That's when she got the hair-brained idea—murder. Brynn sat crisscrossed on the bathroom floor in front of a tall mirror. She held the scissors up next to her, staring at herself in the mirror. *I'm gonna do it. I'm finally gonna do it.* She looked at me in the mirror, all the way from my roots to my ends. She was going to murder me, chop me down into nothing, *me*, the one that's been there through thick and thin. The one that would never split. Murder her mane bitch. She lifted a section of my strands. Was it not enough that people wanted to touch me, control me, and label me? Now, she wanted to get rid of me, too. I didn't fight back. If she wanted a world without me, then she could have it.

When she cut the relaxed parts, only new growth remained. I had my doubts, but amazingly, I was still there. So, I couldn't accuse her of murder anymore. If someone else were telling this story, they would tell you that I was nervously laughing. When I say it got hairy, this time, I mean it literally. Hair was everywhere. It looked like a crime scene. Brynn was stupefied.

"What did I do? Oh God, I look like a dude. I need a wig."

"First of all, they're shears. Secondly, calm down. Thirdly, no, ma'am. You are not smothering me with those bloodless, drab-ass wigs. I need to breathe, honey. You're trying to have us out here looking like one of those 18th-century dukes. No ma'am."

Tears smothered her eyes and a snot bubble formed outside her nose. Her eyes were puffy, and she was sitting there with the shears in her hand, staring at the mirror, unmoving, waiting for something to happen. If she didn't move, she could pretend she was invisible again. She could pretend as if none of today happened. She felt naked like a sphynx, shivering from vulnerability and in need of love.

"Huh?" She turned her head to the right and left like she was in a pool of molasses. She turned around and yanked the shower curtain open, but no one was there. "Who the fuck is talking? I knew it. I've lost my mind."

"Brynn! Say it ain't so. You can hear me now? Finally!" I was elated. Imagine living in a world where no one could hear you. They see you, they look right at you, but they don't listen.

"Whose talking? Who are you?" Here she goes with all these questions.

"Who aren't I? My name is Brair, if that's what you mean."

"Why can't I see you?"

"You're looking right at me. See look. I'll dance for you. I look like a tee-ny-weeny afro-gorgon."

Brynn flicked at me like I was a spider she wanted off.

I was nervous, so I started rambling. "Girl, don't do that. Why are you trying to hurt me today? I'm kidding. Honestly, I thought it would hurt when you cut me, but those must be magical shears that GG gave you. I didn't feel a thing. I feel good. I feel better than good. I feel superb. I could curl an elephant right now. It's like energy is coursing through my follicles. I thought I was alive before. Whew, I'm living. Let's get it."

"What do you want? How did you get here? Wait, it was your voice that I kept hearing?"

"I want the same thing as you. I got here through immaculate conception. Of course, it was me! I've been talking to you for years."

"Brair?"

"Yes?"

"What kind of name is Brair?"

"What kind of name is Brynn?"

Brynn cocked her neck back, offended. She didn't realize I had a smart mouth.

"Brair is for Brynn's hair. Pronounced like Brer, the witty talking rabbit from African folklore, representing enslaved Africans that exacted revenge on white slave owners. Fun fact, the pale potato flesh that stole the stories from slaves and got rich from it is buried here in Atlanta."

Brynn took a deep sigh insinuating I'd given too much information.

I felt stupid. "Don't look at me like that. Let me enjoy this moment. Now I can tell you when I'm thirsty or feeling unraveled. When I feel dirty or need some attention. Wait, did you hear that noise?"

The door of the apartment shut. It was Marc. "Hey, Brynnie."

"He sounds drunk." Only she could hear me, and a good thing too, because I was instigating.

"You drunk, Marc?" Brynn asked.

"Oh shit." He pointed at me. "Where is your hair?"

She was still sitting on the floor when she looked at him standing at the bathroom door and rolled her eyes.

"You look like a man. You look like a dirty bitch-on-freeze. I didn't know I was coming back to a nappy-headed-ho. Give a nigga a heads-up next time."

Brynn stared with bedeviled eyes. The insults heaved from his mouth, except for the occasional intervals when he stopped to chuckle. It was a persecution of her beauty. Hell, of me. She felt like she was being sentenced to loneliness and celibacy.

"Bitch on-freeze? This ignorant motherfucker means Bichon Frisé. He's calling us a dog. When are you getting rid of his ass?" I asked.

"You done, Marc?" Brynn felt self-conscious, she gathered the hair off the floor to distract herself and ignore his onslaughts.

He started making chicken sounds, "buhhcock. Bock-bock. Chickenhead."

Brynn's head jerked back in appall and her left eyebrow rose.

"You ever notice how men have so much to say about how we look? Did you know that a man invented the relaxer? A man came up with the hair chart that we still use today. Men run the largest professional hair show in the world. Hair dye, electric hair dryer, hair curlers, afro pick, man, don't get me wrong. I respect their hustle. I'm just stating facts." I had done it again—info vomit.

"Leave, Marc."

He left the bathroom and went to the den. He flopped on the couch, shoes wet from the rain. Brynn followed him, thinking he was actually going to leave the apartment because that's what she meant.

"Get your nasty ass shoes off my couch and leave, damn."

"Fuck yo' couch, Thing 3." He laughed drunkenly. The couch had shriveled up like the disgruntled mouth of an old man.

"I'm going to go clean the bathroom. When I get back, be gone."

"I know we're not going to sit here and take his shit. I can take care of him with one flick of the wrist, so to speak." I told her.

"Let's not and say we did. Anyway, let's not get violent. That's not a privilege we're allowed. To him, I'll be another bitter black woman."

"Being bitter is just being angry and hurt because of unfair treatment. Tell me you're not rightfully bitter. Plus, you love bitter. You're a bitter bitch. Own that shit. I'ma call you lemon-head from now on. That's your new nickname."

"I'ma let it go—no sense in arguing with a drunk man. I can take his shoes off and let him sleep it off. Then I can talk to him when he gets up." Brynn was still trying to be the bigger person.

"Did you say take his shoes off? For why? What are you, his servant? There ain't nothing to talk about. Let's pick him up by his dirty ass t-shirt and set him in the hallway like the trash he is."

"Let's not and say we did. What would the neighbors think? They'd probably call the police."

"And they can finish what they started. Problem solved."

"Too soon."

Marc called from the living room, "Where's the remote, and why are you always watching this dumb ass show. Angry fuckin' bitches always snappin.'"

"Déjà vu, lemon-head. This feels familiar. It's now or never. I can hear him sloshing off the couch. You know the sound a plunger makes when the shit won't go down? That's him, a shithead."

Brynn never let her unsound thoughts exit her lips. She thought it instead, *letting him leave would be failing him, failing him like I failed Cory... And my dad. No one deserves to be mistreated, even if they have made mistakes. People can change. Brair needs to change. She's telling me what to do. No hair is going to tell* me what to do. She's the reason we're in this mess. She's the reason they look at us like we're crazy. She's the reason they mistreat us.

"Well, that's awkward. I should have mentioned that I can hear your thoughts, my bad. Also, you're the reason you're in this mess. Racism is why they mistreat us. You're talking out the side of your neck, but I'll let it slide."

Brynn smacked her teeth. "You remind me of that talking symbiote from that one movie."

"Which one? Never mind, it doesn't matter. I take that as a compliment for the most part, but I'm no alien. Don't try me." I laughed. "Heads up. Here he go again."

Marc was in the doorway, it was shrinking above him and his body seemed larger under its shape, "who the fuck are you talking to?"

Brynn dismissed him, "You're drunk. You're hearing things."

"Girl, we can handle him." I reminded her.

"With what? You said it yourself, you're a teeny-weeny afro."

"Why are you scared of him?"

"I'm not scared. I'm tired of fighting. I'm done with all his shit. It's not worth the effort."

33
BIG CHOP

August 16, 2020

"**D**id you love him?" Marc asked.

Brynn stopped sweeping, "Yes."

"Do you love me?"

She peered through his eyes, studying his fractured spirit without the urge to repair it. "I loathe you," she answered honestly.

"I bet he doesn't know what that means," I mocked.

Marc grumbled and Brynn continued to sweep. The stream of abuse from his flood of insults was the icing on the cake, she didn't have the words or the emotions to care. He could stay, he could go. She wasn't going to do anything to force it or change it. She became the embodiment of unbothered. She became coarse.

"You fucked him?" He asked.

Back to this again? His ineptitude for a deeper line of questioning amazed me. This led nowhere.

"We've already been over this. I'm not about to do this again."

"I'm right, though, ain't I?" He tried to convince himself.

"You know what? Yeh, I did. I bought a shovel, dug him out of his grave, brought him back to life, fucked him in the dirt, and reburied him. It was the best sex of my life."

"Yeh, you did," he said as if he was psychic.

She grabbed the dustpan and squatted down. "I told you already, I didn't."

He leaned over, grabbing her elbow with his right hand, and holding his pants up with the left, "Lie to me again."

"If you don't get yo grimy ass hands off of me..."

"What you gon' do? You don't have the guts."

She jerked her arm out of his grasp and threw the cut pieces of me away.

"You're ignoring me now? I see how it is."

She emptied the dustpan into the trash and it belched. She tried to push past him. There it was. That lopsided sneer. His body stiffened, making it hard for her to get by. She laughed, so he slammed her against the bathroom door. The door joggled, "Oh, this is funny to you? I'm funny to you?" A look of befuddlement came over her face. He punched a hole in the wall behind her as a show of control, it sent a shiver through the apartment and made the temperature drop, but it only proved that his emotions were out of control.

"You cheated on me and tried to leave me. Then, you tried to kill me. I'm going to show you how that feels."

A downstairs neighbor banged on their ceiling, presumably with a broom, which we heard through the floor.

"I did not try to kill you."

His presence felt taller like it was towering over Brynn. His intention enveloped her psyche. His aura read revenge. She closed her eyes and thought, *maybe I deserve it. Maybe I did try to kill him. Maybe this is my fate—all these murders around me. Maybe, death is trying to find me.*

Finally tired of his ceaseless need to get bodied, I struck because I got *bawdy* for days. Plus, I was boiling inside, overflowing with rage, loss, hurt... And power. A power that I've never felt before. I could feel my roots tingling. I needed a release. Instantly, I grew. I reshaped into a karambit and ran myself across his stomach, slashing him open, and gutting him like a raptor. He took a deep gasp in. Then, I squeezed his insides, giving his lungs the hug that he obviously needed. His body caved in fulfillment. The blood. The blood was everywhere. All over the walls, the rug, the pictures, and the frames in which they hung. Blood dripped. It dropped. It bubbled. With each drip, I cared less. I didn't care. I had two fucks to give. They were donated to the trash, in which the pliant pieces of me now lived. He hurt her. He hurt us. They all did—all of them and their *rights*. I reveled in enjoyment. It was euphoric, but I needed to get him out of my hair.

Blood splattered across Brynn's face, and the sound of his body hitting the floor startled her eyes open. "You might be done fighting, lemon-head, but that doesn't mean you can't protect yourself," I said.

Brynn stared at him on the floor. She was reminded of her mother, reminded of Ian, reminded of Cory. "Wh...What...Why did you do this?" Except this wasn't that. This time, there was no running.

"I protected you because clearly, you can't do it yourself." I felt justified.

The neighbor banged again, but only once this time. Brynn picked up the phone, fumbling with it in the air.

"I know you're not about to call the police. If you want to blame someone, don't call the responsible party. Have you no self-preservation?"

"I'm calling GG."

"The other part of the responsible party?" I tried to influence her.

"GG had a similar situation before." We knew that from *the* memories.

The phone rang. She propped it on her left shoulder and grabbed the first thing she saw, his black hoodie. The phone rang. She covered his face. She couldn't look him in the eyes. The phone rang. Failure stared back at her. GG didn't answer.

"What do I do? Think, think, think." She paced in her bedroom, talking to herself, "I have to call the police. It was self-defense."

"Yeh, and when they ask why he has a gaping hole in his stomach, tell them your symbiote got hungry. They'll write you a ticket and carry the body out for you...NOT! Are you crazy?"

The phone rang. She pressed it against her chest for a quick moment, as she tried to will things her way. "Please be GG." She answered, "Hello?"

"Hi, Miss Brown. This is the after-hours resident on duty. We received a complaint of loud noises and arguing." The resident chuckled, "they said it sounded like someone was dying up there. Is everything okay?"

I turned into Inspector-Hair, "How does death sound when there's no scream? She said up there as if it was the neighbor down below that complained. I don't mean to be dramatic, but we are going to have to take care of her. You still like helping folks, don't ya?"

The resident waited for a response. "Ma'am, are you there?"

Brynn had zoned out. "Yeh, what did you say?"

"I asked if are you okay. Do I need to call the police?"

"No. No, everything is good. I tripped and fell. Thanks for checking on me." Click.

She stumbled to the linen closet for every towel, sheet, washcloth, and fabric available. She got the bleach from atop the dryer, a bucket from her storage closet, and that purple smell-good cleaner from under the kitchen sink.

"What are you doing with all that? That's not how you clean up the departed."

"Why didn't I hear his scream?" Brynn got on her hands and knees, letting the blood soak into the towels.

"That's what you're thinking about right now?"

"You brought it up, Brair." Brynn's eye twitched. *Oh my God, am I really talking to my hair right now? This is stupid.*

Brynn layered the towels.

"Would you have preferred to hear a scream? You and everyone else living in this complex? That's some serial killer shit, lemon-head, wanting to hear someone scream. But... you try screaming with someone squeezing your lungs from the inside and crushing your larynx. Tell me how that goes."

There was a tapping sound. "Brynn. Stop. Did you hear that?"

Brynn froze, looking around the apartment. "Hear what?"

Tap-Tap. "Someone's knocking at the door."

"Police! Open up." The knocks got louder, then abruptly stopped.

"Oh my God, they're going to bust in the door. Oh my God. Oh my God," Brynn jumped up, frantic. When she didn't hear the cop, and the door wasn't busted open, she tip-toed over.

On the other side of the peephole, Brynn saw three women. Their backs were facing her. A woman's locs were flowing, almost floating, waving like they were underwater. She was doing something with her hair. The smell of vanilla seeped under the door. She heard them whisper, and she gasped. All three women looked at the door simultaneously.

34
TWA

August 16, 2020

Brynn eagerly unlocked the door. Her mouth flung open. There was a police officer lying on the breezeway floor. I couldn't tell if he should be counting sheep or pushing daisies. His right arm was suspended in the air, extended out toward the women like he had been pleading for help. It looked like rigor mortis, but that usually takes hours. He'd only knocked on the door moments ago. The weird thing was, his eyes were opened. Those inbred eyeballs indolently rolled in my direction. Brynn looked at the three women with questioning eyes. She didn't want to ask anything yet, fearing the neighbors might hear.

"Close your mouth before a fly flies in," Tina teased. "Let us in."

Brynn stepped aside, "Mrs. Kruger? Is that you? What are you doing here? How do you know my family?" The last time I saw her, she barely had any grey hair. Now, it was almost covered in it. Mixed in were different shades of brown like burnt metal. I'd never seen anything like it.

Mrs. Kruger responded, "Don't make me feel old. Call me Ella."

Aunt Tina interrupted and scooted Brynn out of the way, "Your Aunt Casey saw what happened. Mama was already in the car, ready." GG closed the door behind them.

"You're going to leave that cop out there like that?" Brynn gestured toward Tina since she seemed to be running things, despite GG being the eldest.

"I didn't touch him. Did you touch him?" Tina grinned. "Ella, do you mind getting started on cleanup?"

"Started?" Ella smirked, "you say that like you planned to help."

"Uhh, he looks dead to me," she stared at Marc. "Ain't much I can do now," she flipped her locs behind her shoulder and sat on the couch. GG stood by the door, leaning on her cane. Auntie reminded me of myself. She was sassy. I liked her, but she seemed laid back, cool and collected. This wasn't the impression I had of her before today. Maybe we shouldn't have assumed things about her because she looks like mom. Ella bent forward and shook her hair like a white girl in a shampoo commercial. A ring of blue fire crept from the tips of her kinky corkscrew curls, leaving behind smoldering ash in its path until it fizzled out at her roots. Her hair had morphed into strands of ash. Embers fluttered around her like twinkling stars.

"What is this? What's going on?" Brynn looked at each of them.

"You're going to want to stay back for this one," Tina patted the couch that had grown back to normal size since they arrived, filling itself with warmth. Brynn sat down. I could see Marc's body in the hallway from the couch. Ella scoped the scene, nodding at the blood on the walls, tallying the pieces of Marc, taking note of every detail. She rolled her shoulders back and took a deep sigh.

"Brynn, it's so nice to see you again," Ella said sarcastically. "I'm no therapist, but I'm starting to notice a pattern."

Tina raised an eyebrow.

Ella tapped her bottom lip, "What was his name? That kid from school."

"Ian," I said to Brynn.

Brynn repeated it with an unsure tone, "Ian?"

Ella took her finger from her lip and pointed at Brynn, "Yeh, him."

"Wait, what happened now?" Tina asked.

Ella looked at Brynn, "My bad. I thought she knew. I'll let you tell her."

Brynn held out her hand if to say go ahead, "no, that's okay." She was relieved that Aunt Tina asked because as I said way earlier, that day was foggy for Brynn.

She didn't remember much, and even though we had our memories back, GG didn't do a great job of it. This particular day was a memory that felt tampered with memories of GG's, like two timelines overlapping. Ella waggled her head slightly so the fiery ash landed on the chunks of Marc, a tiny fire engulfed them until they turned to dust. Ella cleaned as she narrated back to the day I fell in love. Brynn watched her work, entranced.

"So, it was the end of the day and this kid, Ian, was bothering Brynn. After all of the students left, I was trying to calm her down, but in the midst of all that, I got called to the office. End-of-school-year things and whatnot. My class was in a trailer next to the school. I was making my way to the building but barely got into the side-door when something told me to turn around. I looked through the glass window of the door and saw Ian go back into the trailer. He was a sneaky lil' something, so I waited a minute for him to come back out. That's when another teacher walked up to me. We used to call her Chatty Cathy because she would never shut up and before I knew it, a few minutes had gone by. I hurried to the trailer and there was Ian, laid out on the floor. Brynn was nowhere to be found. It looked kind of like this, but less blood." She motioned with her fiery hair at Marc's body, letting a few embers clean up the splatter.

Tina mumbled a sound, "mmhmm."

Ella continued. "Well, Ian wasn't dead, and thank goodness because how was I going to explain a missing child after I cleaned up the body? It looked like whatever got to him wasn't just an angry little girl throwing punches. And if it was my seemingly innocent student..." She looked at Brynn, "...Then there was something more going on." Ella stepped over Marc's limp arm on the floor, setting more pieces of him aflame. "To answer your previous question, Brynn, I met your family when I went to your parents' house the following Monday to check on you. Well, that's how I met Georgia. She was there packing, and we got to talking. At that point, I only told her that you got into a fight with a boy in school. But then she told me that you had come home that same day and something even worse had happened. Georgia couldn't talk about it in detail then, but I got the point. We put two and two together, realizing that we all shared the same… Strengths. Since then, we call on each other for help here and there. Grab lunch every blue moon."

Tina avoided eye contact with Brynn, "You can't keep hurting people, Brynn."

Brynn slumped in her seat. *I'm not hurting people, I heal people. I help people.* She felt judged. *Is this a pattern? Am I angry? Why do I hurt people when I'm supposed to be helping them? I don't mean to hurt people. That's not who I am.*

"Lemon-head, they're not perfect either. Ask them."

Brynn probed Aunt Tina, "Haven't you ever killed someone? Don't you hurt people?"

GG repositioned her feet, not joining the conversation. She knew where this was going. Tina looked at Brynn, feeling tried, "Jump off your high horse, sweetie." Tina pointed with her head. "I'm looking at someone dead on your floor right now." Brynn didn't want to think it because she knew I could hear. She wondered not only of her immorality but of mine. This wasn't who she was. This was who I was. I didn't suppress my emotions. I got revenge. I didn't feel an obligation to help others. I did what was best for me. She was becoming more like me. It was time to leave that selfless act behind and help herself. Getting rid of Marc, and I hate to say it but getting rid of her mother, got her what she wanted.

"I forgave you for taking my sister. That was a mistake. You were coming into your powers. Accidents happen. But this was a choice." She pointed at Marc again. "I understand why you did it but it's not a choice you want to keep making…Anyway," Tina huffed, "I don't kill people. Let's put a positive spin on what I do. I provide people the means to step back and look at themselves. It's an opportunity to sit down, be quiet, and rest. Or, in that cop's case outside, a chance to mind his business. I induce disease, contagions, pathogens, and sickness. All that stuff people are afraid of, sure, but on the bright side, they usually get better."

Georgia was still leaning on her cane. She kept quiet, knowing if she took Tina's side she would be the pot calling the kettle black.

Brynn clarified. "You're like the gun, and the bullet is the sickness."

Tina crossed her legs, "something like that."

It got silent. They all focused on the ring of fire sluggishly consuming Marc's body. Bit by bit, he turned to ash. She would miss him, but the weight of responsibility had lifted. The obligation to fix destroyed. The duty to help dissipated.

"Good riddance," I said heartily.

Brynn's eyes looked upward at me. "Don't be like that."

GG and Tina looked at each other confused. Tina asked, "Who are you talking to?"

"My hair. Y'all's hair don't talk to you? I thought it came with the powers."

GG, Tina, and Ella all looked at each other, concerned. Ella turned back around. "I've said enough. I'm going to stay out of this one."

Tina sighed, "Some of us can communicate with our hair. It's rare, but it happens. I've heard the hair takes on a character. It has emotions and free will. It does whatever it wants. It's referred to as bad hair."

Brynn interjected, "So, we are witches?"

"I thought millennials didn't like labels," Tina mocked.

"I'm not a millennial. I'm a zillenial."

Tina side-eyed Brynn, "One of the worst of them all was Nandipha. She had the most beautiful curl pattern and took great care of her hair, moisturizing it, showering it with attention, and keeping it covered in pure silk. Her hair was never tangled and always manageable—everything you wished your hair to be. She was being courted by a man, the captain of a dynasty in Griqualand West, South Africa. He was a narcissistic aberration to mankind. But, knowing she had powers, he said he would marry her if she stood alongside him in battle. She agreed, so long as she only needed to help when he was in imminent danger. One day, he brought her to the edge of a cliff and, as they looked over at the tents of a thousand sleeping men, he asked her to kill them, all of them. Granted, the men had planned to attack him the next day, but they hadn't. It was against her moral compass. She disagreed with his tactics, thinking it should be a fair fight. No one knows why, but her hair decided otherwise. All one thousand men were crushed—every single one—simultaneously. She was untouchable. I'm not saying her hair was bad, but usually, it did bad things."

"She sounds overpowering." Brynn was both astounded and critical. My-my, how the tables have turned.

"Correction. She sounds strong." Said Tina.

"I'm confused. You said she was bad."

Tina shook her head, "No, I said she did a bad thing. Well, her hair did."

"Maybe it was an accident?"

Tina tilted her head as if looking over a pair of invisible glasses. GG pointed with her cane. Regrettably, she had to know, "Was this your doing or your hair?"

Brynn exclaimed, "He was about to hurt me—"

"Brynn?" GG asked again.

Brynn became wary. After receiving memories from GG, she knew people weren't always who they claimed to be. "What did Aunt Casey say? She saw the whole thing, right? Spying on me with her magic eyes, or whatever."

"I'm not asking her. I'm asking you."

Brynn appealed. "I mean…. I am my hair, and my hair is me. We are one. Would you rather we're dead right now instead of him?"

GG countered, "I would have rather you cut the cape before this happened. I told you, if you hadn't been trying to be a superhero, you wouldn't be in this shit. You can't save the world. You're one person."

Tina hugged Brynn because she knew of all the things GG was, a hugger wasn't one of them, "We get it. You're the only one that helped him. You were there for him when he needed you the most. When you needed him, he wasn't there, and there was no Brynn to help Brynn. You can't heal yourself, but you need to heal. You felt vulnerable, lonely… Betrayed. Put the oxygen mask on yourself first. Breathe. We're here to help you. Now, you have someone. We got you." Tina rubbed Brynn's back in circles and Brynn embraced the hug. She closed her eyes as they started to water and, for a second, pretended Aunt Tina was her mother. She pretended she was back at her old home, and instead of arguing, they hugged and found a way to get through it together. She wiped the tears from her eyes.

Tina looked over her shoulder. "Ella, how's it going over there?"

"Ashes to ashes. Dust to dust. Getting this blood up won't be easy since it's intertwined in the carpet, and I'm not trying to set this place on fire. I'll have to focus, so I'll need y'all to stop yapping or leave."

"Right, let's go. Brynn, grab some of your things," Tina directed.

As they walked out the door, Brynn asked, "What about the neighbor downstairs?"

"I took care of her," said GG.

"GG, you took care of her?"

"Girl, she's fine. Come on."

The door shut behind them, and they heard sirens. Brynn stopped. GG and Tina froze in place. The sound got louder. Tina looked the cop in his eyes. He could only move them slightly, but they screamed for help. Her locs floated as if to ready herself. Then the sirens became quiet, passing out of range. Brynn heaved a sigh, "The police pass by here often." She stood next to the cop, talking to GG and Tina, "We're going to leave him here?" Tina shut the door, "You weren't worried about leaving folks when you left that boy in class." Brynn threw her overnight bag on her shoulder, stuttering, "I... I... He..." Tina scorned, "he, he, hell. You're lucky Ella was there. So, don't worry about it. She's going to get rid of your mess... Again." Tina gestured for Brynn to keep walking down the breezeway but Brynn didn't move.

"We already feel horrible," she looked down, fidgeting with her phone charger. "Don't rub it in."

I liked that we were a team now, but that wasn't completely true. I didn't feel horrible.

"Wait, Ella's not going to turn this cop to dust, is she?" Brynn asked.

"If she does, tell her I'd like some leftovers. Pork sounds good." I joked.

Tina brushed off her tone. "I can't undo what I've done. Since your mom and I were twins, she had the power to cure. She was my other half, but I hear you can heal, so help him if you want." Tina shrugged, "The choice is yours. It's in your hands... Well, your hair," she chuckled, shaking her head.

"Brynn, do you want to help him?" GG asked.

"No."

Of all the millions of books worldwide, I'm so glad you discovered this one. That's magical! If you'd like to know when I release a new book, instead of leaving it to chance, sign up for my newsletter. I'll send you an email on publication.

Visit **www.angeliqueinostine.com/yes**